Captive Brides
SOLANGE AYRE

Ellora's Cave
Romantica Publishing

One Thousand Brides

"We require wives. A review of the populated planets in your region revealed that Earth females are the closest genetically to our species. Thus we have decided to take one thousand human females with us."

As these words are broadcast over Earth media, Janis Stone blacks out. She awakens on an alien colonization ship, one of a thousand human women destined to become Brides of the Terilian colonists.

At first outraged by the kidnapping, Jan soon finds herself intrigued by Delos, the Terilian doctor who serves as liaison to the human Brides. Despite his pointed, furry ears and the pelt down his back, Delos' muscular physique and wonderful scent draw Jan like catnip attracting a feline. The two embark on a sensual journey, exploring their species' sexual compatibility.

But their new love is threatened when a higher-ranked male desires Jan. As she plans a mass wedding for the thousand Brides, she dreads the upcoming "Spring Running", the mysterious rite where Terilians will mate with their Brides. Will the wrong groom claim her?

Bride Reborn

Snow Jarrett, suffering from Multiple Sclerosis, blacks out and awakens on an alien colonization ship. The Terilians, who lost all their females to a deadly virus, have kidnapped a thousand human women to be their Brides.

Although her MS has been cured, Snow needs therapy to make her muscles strong again. Her physical therapist, Ryus of the Silver Pelt, is the most gorgeous male she's ever met. Ryus provides a sensual mixture of sexual and physical therapy that soon has her eager to become his Bride.

The ship's council declares that if Snow is not strong enough to bring a male to climax, she will be exiled. Ryus, afraid to lose another loved one, tries to resist his overwhelming desire for the courageous Earth woman who has captured his heart.

An Ellora's Cave Romantica Publication

www.ellorascave.com

Captive Brides

ISBN 9781419960901
ALL RIGHTS RESERVED.
One Thousand Brides Copyright © 2007 Solange Ayre.
Bride Reborn Copyright © 2009 Solange Ayre.
Edited by Helen Woodall.
Cover art by Syneca.

This book printed in the U.S.A. by Jasmine-Jade Enterprises, LLC.

Trade paperback publication May 2010

The terms Romantica® and Quickies® are registered trademarks of Ellora's Cave Publishing.

With the exception of quotes used in reviews, this book may not be reproduced or used in whole or in part by any means existing without written permission from the publisher, Ellora's Cave Publishing, Inc.® 1056 Home Avenue, Akron OH 44310-3502.

Warning: The unauthorized reproduction or distribution of this copyrighted work is illegal. Criminal copyright infringement, including infringement without monetary gain, is investigated by the FBI and is punishable by up to 5 years in federal prison and a fine of $250,000.
(http://www.fbi.gov/ipr/)

This book is a work of fiction and any resemblance to persons, living or dead, or places, events or locales is purely coincidental. The characters are productions of the author's imagination and used fictitiously.

CAPTIVE BRIDES
Solange Ayre
ಐ

ONE THOUSAND BRIDES
~9~

BRIDE REBORN
~101~

ONE THOUSAND BRIDES

Dedication

☙

Dedicated to my wonderful critique partners (in alphabetical order by last name): Christy C., Edwina C., Ellen D., Dianne H., Chris N., and Nancy S. Thank you, darlings! I promise we'll have a lovely house party on Ayriana as soon as I get back to Earth.

Trademarks Acknowledgement

☙

The author acknowledges the trademarked status and trademark owners of the following wordmarks mentioned in this work of fiction:

BBC: British Broadcasting Corporation

Macy's: Macy's Department Stores, Inc.

PowerPoint: Microsoft Corporation

Chapter One

What sadist put a bakery next to a bridal shop? Jan tried to ignore the enticing aroma of fresh bread as she hurried into Bev's Bridal Boutique. Her rumbling stomach reminded her that she'd had nothing but soup for lunch.

"I'm Janis Stone," she said, approaching the counter. "I'd like to try my dress on, please."

In the dressing room, the smiling attendant helped her into the longline corset with its built-in bra. Through strenuous exercise and dieting, Jan had managed to lose thirty-two pounds over the last three months. She said a little prayer as the attendant lowered the clouds of white satin over her head. *Please God, make it fit this time.*

"I'm sorry," the attendant said. "I just can't get the last two buttons done—the ones at your waist. I wish you'd let me order the size sixteen."

Jan shook her head, thinking of the day when she and Gary had chosen the dress. "All that white makes you look enormous," he'd said, frowning. "My God, Jan, my mother had five children and still wears a size six."

She'd come close to calling off the wedding. He'd apologized—but the remark still rankled. She'd decided to go on a diet.

After all, she was thirty-nine years old, ordinary looking and a little too heavy. No wonder she'd never been married. Gary was her last chance.

She'd pictured herself married since age ten. When she finally received an engagement ring, it had been such a pleasure to show it to the other women at work, to e-mail her old college roommates, to call her mother—who'd cried with joy.

For years she'd brought gifts to her friends' wedding showers. Exclaimed over their dresses. Danced at their weddings while keeping a sharp eye out for the Mr. Right who always seemed to be partnering younger, more petite women.

Finally, after all these years, it was her turn. She could hardly wait for her big day. The candle-lit ceremony, the friends and family from out of town, her attendants in their pale pink. She was looking forward to every wonderfully mundane detail.

Even The Chicken Dance.

Jan hummed along with the music being piped through the store. Surely those last two buttons would close if she went on a liquid diet for the next week...

A harsh burst of static came over the speaker. The sound hurt Janis' ears and she winced.

"People of Earth." The arrogant voice sounded much like a BBC announcer. "I am Primus Taddus of the Black-Striped Pelt, a council member of the colonization ship *Ecstasy of Generations*."

Jan turned to the attendant, who looked every bit as puzzled as Jan felt. "It's got to be a joke," Jan whispered.

The voice continued, "Necessity has compelled us to seek your help. In the fourth year of our seven-year journey, a short stay on a planetary satellite exposed us to an unknown virus. To our great sorrow, every one of our females perished.

"We require wives. A review of the populated planets in your region revealed that Earth females are the closest genetically to our species. Thus we have decided to take one thousand human females with us.

"We carefully chose fertile females under age forty, childless and not presently pair-bonded. Do not be concerned for your compatriots—they will have rich and rewarding lives in a far more enlightened society than your own.

"We regret the necessity for our actions and thank you most sincerely for your time and trouble."

As soon as the voice cut off, dizziness flooded Janis' senses. She tried to catch hold of the chair in the dressing room as she fell to her knees. As everything went dark, she thought, *If I tear this dress, I'll shoot myself.*

* * * * *

Pleasure danced down every nerve, from the top of her head to the soles of her feet. Jan moaned deep in her throat. She wanted to stretch luxuriously, like a cat basking in sunlight but sleep held her immobile. A tingling sensation pulsed through her, arousing her nipples. They grew heavy and engorged, as though a lover had suckled them for an hour. The sensual awakening flew down to her pelvis, which suffused with heat as delight rippled through her. Her clit swelled and her pussy ached to be filled.

Please, she begged, *please don't stop. I'll die if you stop.*

The wonderful titillation went on and on, varying in intensity, increasing the thrill. The teasing concentrated on her clit. She was about to explode when the stimulation switched to her hot, slick channel. Moving hard, like a vigorous lover, the sensation then muted to the tentative touch of one finger. Every nerve spiked to attention, starving for more.

Suddenly a thousand tiny tongues lapped at her, stimulating her nether lips, her clit and the tight rosebud of her ass.

A headlong rush toward orgasm, like speeding down the world's longest, smoothest roller coaster. Everything opened at once, her pussy welcoming all sensations, drowning in them, overflowing. She tumbled through huge waves of pleasure that left her shuddering and swooning as they receded. She drew in a great gasp of air and her eyes flew open.

She'd just had an incredibly intense orgasm...from her mind alone. No one was close enough to touch her, yet her pussy pulsed as though the world's greatest lover had given her the world's most intense fucking.

Where am I? What's happening to me? She shivered, her heart pounding with fear.

The narrow bed, the bright, recessed lights, the smell of antiseptic were all familiar.

Is it a hospital? That guy looks a little strange, though. Am I on some weird hallucinogen?

A man lounged against the doorway, studying what looked like a handheld electronic device. He glanced up. "Janis Stone. You're awake." Smiling, he approached with catlike grace.

He was slender and tall, well over six feet in height. His long hair, hanging slightly past his shoulders, was a mass of dark brown varied with lighter patches of tan.

Two furry peaks poked through his hair at the top of his head. *Bad hair day?* she wondered. *No, those are his ears. He's not a man. He's an alien.*

The fog began to clear from her brain. She strained to remember the last thing she'd heard. Her breathing quickened.

"Secondus Delos of the Tawny-Spotted Pelt. Your physician." His pale blue eyes studied her. Jan focused on them, noting they were rounder than human eyes, with long, narrow pupils. Still, they held a kindly expression. "How are you feeling?" His deep, rich voice flowed over her like warm cream, calming and soothing her.

How am I feeling? After having the best orgasm of my life? But I doubt he's asking about my sexual health.

"Disoriented," she said at last. Her voice was hoarse, as though she hadn't spoken in a long time.

"Not surprising. Some of that's the pain medication. Rest assured, you're going to be feeling much better soon."

The doctor wore a sleeveless blue tunic that revealed the powerful muscles of his shoulders and arms. Sturdy legs were encased in dark blue tights.

He sat casually on the side of her bed and took her wrist in his large hand.

He's an alien and he's touching me. Her trembling increased.

"Don't worry, I'm just taking your pulse." His smile gave her a warm feeling, until she noticed his fang-shaped incisors.

In spite of the fact that he had two eyes, a nose and a mouth, something about his face didn't quite add up to "human". Maybe it was his small nose. Or the stiff hairs under his nose that were more like a cat's whiskers than a man's mustache.

"I've been worried about you," he continued. "You took the Transition hard. Most of the other Brides have been awake for two or three days."

Other Brides? "How long have I been here?" she asked, her alarm growing.

"Seven weeks." He grasped her shoulder with a comforting hand. "Do you remember the broadcast? Do you know why you're here?"

In the back of her mind she'd been aware of the knowledge but hadn't wanted to face it. "So it's all true then?" She wasn't sure whether she should scream hysterically or break into sobs.

None of that will do any good. Just stay calm. She took deep breaths and tried to relax.

"It's true." His eyes contained attractive little flecks of darker blue. He leaned closer and she received an enticing whiff of his scent. Some of it was clean, healthy male but there was an underlying addition…cocoa, maybe? Whatever the scent, she wanted to lick him all over. *Lick him? That's got to be the drugs.*

"I'm sure you have questions. Go ahead and ask. I've been appointed Official Liaison to the Brides."

Official liaison or kidnapping conspirator? "How nice for you. Did you get a pay raise?"

A twitch of Dr. Delos' mouth showed that he'd caught her sarcasm. "Our economic incentives don't work quite the same way as in your culture. Anyway the answer is no. I volunteered solely for the pleasure of working with beautiful females."

Too bad you got stuck with me, then. "The person who spoke on the broadcast said you wanted wives." Was she really expected to marry an alien? Someone like the doctor, with furry ears?

To her shock she realized the idea intrigued her. *Maybe it has something to do with that unusual wake-up call.*

"Yes, you were all brought here to marry us." Was there an apologetic note in his voice?

Jan strove to remember everything from the announcement. "He said your females died."

"All of us were ill after the landing on Rinora-3. Two-thirds of our males recovered but our females..." He closed his eyes briefly. "I'm sorry. It's difficult to talk about."

In spite of his nonhuman features, she was able to read the pain in his expression. "Were *you* married?" she asked.

"In our culture, all adults are married. I understand humans are different. We were shocked to find a thousand lovely females who were not yet pair-bonded."

"How did you know we weren't pair-bonded?"

"In choosing our Brides, we uploaded data on many females from the most technologically advanced areas of Earth. You're the result of an extensive selection process. One of a thousand, chosen out of millions."

Just like hitting the lottery. "You know what? That makes me feel *so much better* about being brought here against my will."

He didn't respond to her jibe but answered seriously. "I know this is hard for you. You'll understand more tomorrow."

There's got to be a way to escape. I'll think about it when I'm not so tired. "What's happening tomorrow?"

"The council's planning a meeting with all the Brides. I'd like to get you walking around before that. Are you ready to sit up?"

She almost answered that she wanted to go to sleep and never wake up again. But she didn't want to look weak in front of him, so she nodded.

"Good. I'll help you." He put his arm around her shoulders. A strand of his long hair brushed against her cheek. His wonderful scent drew her like catnip attracting a feline.

A sudden vision came to her of cuddling against his chest. What would he do? Hold her, murmur soothing words? The idea was so intriguing that she almost cast herself into his arms.

More likely he'd give me a tranquilizer. Better behave myself.

"Here we go." He raised her to a sitting position. Her head swam and the room spun like rows of fruit whirling in a slot machine.

"Dizzy!" she gasped.

"Don't worry, I've got you. Take deep breaths."

Gradually the room steadied. In spite of herself, she drew comfort from Dr. Delos' steady grip. Although he was an alien he also seemed to be a caring doctor.

She wore a plain yellow tunic that was embarrassingly sheer, considering her nipples were still peaking. Couldn't he have provided a decent hospital gown?

"Bed—raise back to support patient," he commanded. The bed obeyed him and the doctor released her. Jan suppressed an instant feeling of loss.

A twinge in her midriff brought her hand to her stomach.

"I took the feeding tube out yesterday," the doctor explained.

"Feeding tube!"

"My examinations revealed that you were malnourished." His voice filled with pride as he added, "You've gained ten pounds while you've been under my care."

"Thanks a whole hell of a lot," she muttered. Another question surfaced in her mind. "How is it we're able to understand each other?"

"My team and I implanted brain chips when you first arrived. We're actually speaking Terilian. Your brain's translating it into English."

If this wasn't some horribly fantastic dream, she was in deep shit. Unless she and the other women could convince the aliens otherwise, none of them would see Earth again. She'd never see her mother or brothers again, never see her girlfriends.

Or Gary. She wondered why the thought of never seeing Gary again didn't cause more than a tiny pang.

Stay tough, Jan. Folding her arms across her chest, she said, "So the mass kidnapping was successful. When does the mass rape take place?"

Concern filled his eyes. "Rape is impossible in our culture. When the Spring Running takes place, you Earthian females will joyfully accept your new husbands."

Don't count on it. "What is this Spring Running?"

He stood. "Don't concern yourself with that now. We'll speak more tomorrow." As he turned to go, he added, "Just tell the bed to return to the sleep position when you want to lie down again. And don't worry—you'll attract one of our high-status males with your great beauty."

*****

Delos frowned as he rode the shuttle back to his quarters. Two years without a mate had been difficult. Worse than difficult. Almost impossible.

Still, that didn't excuse his unprofessional behavior with Janis Stone. He hoped none of the council had been monitoring Sick Bay when he'd sat on her bed.

He'd been overwhelmingly tempted, determined to breathe in more of her aroma. The multi-layered scents of the new Brides had made it difficult to treat them. He remembered how Hannus, one of the orderlies, had fainted during Janis' brain-chip operation, overwhelmed by his hormonal response to her.

Delos sighed. He'd been fascinated by Janis' scent from his first day of studying her chemistry, administering the proper drugs to guide her through the Transition. She'd been an enticing medley of interesting aromas. Her hair had smelled different from her skin. Some of it was her, some an artificial overlay.

As the weeks passed, her natural scent predominated, a deep, woodsy smell that belonged to her alone. It brought back memories of his home planet, Teril. He recalled running through the forest as a youth, the sun dim through the mists and the green and red fronds brushing against his legs as he chased his brothers.

But most intoxicating of all was the distinctive aroma of her sex. He shivered, recalling how greatly her scent had intensified when he'd tested her orgasmic strength with the electronic stimulator. If he licked her, would that lovely skin between her breasts taste different from that smooth skin just above her female pelt?

His organ had hardened and lengthened while he spoke to her. Had she noticed? Probably not, since his tunic was loose and flowing. If only he could have her for his own, he would ask for nothing else in this life. He imagined her opening herself to him, the sweet, glistening folds ready for him to plunge into. She would scream with delight…

Don't do this to yourself, Del. You know very well she can never be yours.

Chapter Two

✼

The next time Jan woke, a large, gruff orderly named Hannus helped her out of bed. Leaning on his arm, she took tentative steps around the small room. Her legs felt rubbery, as though her muscles had disappeared.

Hannus brought her a meal on a tray—ten miniscule bowls, each filled with a different delicious food. Most of them tasted meaty, although one had a cornmeal consistency.

"Secondus Delos says to eat all you can. If you want more of anything, you have only to ask," the orderly told her.

Thoughts of her diet flitted through her mind. *Hell, what does it matter now?* She finished everything on the tray.

Hannus gave her a clean tunic to wear. Much like Delos', it was sleeveless, except that it was bright red and reached to her knees. Accompanying it were soft red shoes, somewhat like ballet slippers. "I don't get tights?"

Hannus looked shocked. "Females never wear tights."

He held up a mirror so that she could see herself. Jan blushed. Her large breasts were clearly visible through the sheer top, as well as the dark triangle of curls at the juncture of her thighs. She felt naked and exposed and her embarrassment was enhanced by the aide's frankly appreciative glance.

"What happened to the clothes I had when I was brought here?" *Not that I want to run around in white satin…*

"In storage. Besides, Secondus Delos was right." Hannus' eyes glowed with enthusiasm. "This color enhances your unique beauty." She felt as though he were standing too close as he took a deep breath. *Is he…smelling me?*

"The council is addressing the Brides in a few minutes," he continued. "If I help you, can you walk fifty feet to the Great Hall?"

Excitement ran through her at the thought of seeing other women again. She held out her arm and he took it reverently, as though she were a queen.

They moved slowly through a long corridor. Jan narrowed her eyes to look at the walls, which showed twisted trees with red leaves and green and aqua ferns. If the illusion hadn't ended with a plain violet ceiling, she would have almost imagined herself in a forest.

Most of the other Brides were already seated in the Great Hall when Jan came in. She stared at hundreds of faces, noting that all races of Earth were represented. The women wore sheer tunics in a glad rainbow of colors, from deepest blue to sunshine yellow to pale pink.

None of them were slender. Everyone she looked at was her size or slightly bigger. Could this possibly mean that the aliens prized large women?

The shrill sound of a thousand women chattering to each other filled the cavernous room and for a moment Jan had the impulse to put her hands over her ears.

Funny, she'd never noticed before that each woman in a crowd had her own particular scent.

Jan dropped gratefully onto a padded stool and looked up at the front of the room, where a row of aliens knelt on similar stools, murmuring to each other. Five of them wore gray. Their bodies were decorated with copper or silver — arm bracelets, ankle bracelets. Several of them wore necklaces.

At the far left, a little apart from the rest, Secondus Delos looked out toward the Brides. Clad only in a dark-green tunic and tights, he seemed younger than the other aliens. He caught her eye and smiled. Relieved to see a familiar face, Jan smiled back.

An earsplitting whistle sounded and one of the males in gray came to his feet. He was a tall, big-shouldered fellow with long black hair streaked with gray at the temples.

"Welcome, Brides. I am Primus Taddus of the Black-Striped Pelt. We're so glad you've joined us on the *Ecstasy of Generations* colonization ship."

Like we had a choice? Jan thought wryly.

"While I realize it's a shock for you to part from your families and friends, I'm sure that leaving your primitive, polluted planet will soon be seen as a blessing. In another year, we'll make planetfall. You'll be a vital part of our exciting colonization venture."

Exciting – or dangerous?

"We chose you as our Brides because you come from the same Forerunner race as our ancestors. We already share ninety-eight percent of the same genetics. In addition, we find you almost as beautiful as our own females.

"Most of you have already received explanations from your doctors but let me quickly review what's been done to you. The doctors have administered drugs designed to give you a complete cellular overhaul."

What the hell? Jan tensed.

"The changes are subtle but you are now much more like Terilian females." His cocky voice implied they'd been given a wonderful gift. "Your sense of smell is enhanced, as is your hearing. You'll find, in the weeks to come, greater muscular strength. Most importantly, you'll be able to bear healthy young for your destined husbands."

Ignoring the angry murmuring that swelled through the hall, Primus Taddus continued, "A little thought, a little reflection, will soon show you how lucky you are to be lifted out of your primitive lives and allowed to share our glorious Terilian heritage—"

Jan couldn't stand it any longer. Shooting to her feet, she ignored the dizziness that assailed her. "How dare you? How dare you speak as though we should be grateful? You kidnapped us! On Earth, that's considered a *crime*."

As if her outburst had set off a Roman candle, a hundred other women jumped to their feet.

"We don't want to bear your young!"

"Take us home, you bastards!"

"We'll never marry you!"

Delos rose lithely and went to speak to Taddus. The two males' conversation seemed to grow more angry by the second. Rising, Taddus stared threateningly into Delos' eyes. Delos leaned forward and made a chopping motion with his right hand.

Delos must have won the argument, for when the whistle sounded again, he stepped closer to the Brides to speak.

"Primus Taddus has made an inspiring speech but he left one thing out—how very badly we need you." Delos' voice, in contrast to Taddus', was filled with sorrow. "Without wives, our mission is doomed. We can't colonize a planet by ourselves, with males only."

"Then go back to your home planet!" a furious blonde shouted.

Delos turned his head slowly, his glance taking in all the Brides. "The council didn't want to reveal this to you but I'll tell you anyway. Humans can go for years without mating. Terilian males can't.

"We've been without wives for two years. We're at the end of our endurance. We cannot survive the four-year journey back to Teril. We'd all be dead before we arrived."

The furious whispers in the room ceased.

"Janis Stone said we committed a crime. We did—but only because our very survival is at stake. People will do almost anything to survive. This is true on Earth and true on Teril. Someday, perhaps you'll forgive us."

Jan was still angry but Delos' apologetic tone stirred something within her. Yes, she understood that they'd wanted to survive.

But forgive them? She wasn't so sure of that.

Delos continued, "In the meantime, we hope you'll find happiness in mating with us at the Spring Running. The cellular overhaul has made you respond to Terilian male pheromones. The Running is a joyous event in Terilian lives, a great pleasure that all anticipate."

Taddus stood again. "Enough, Delos! No more talk of sacred things."

Delos inclined his head and changed the subject. "I've heard questions as I tended you Brides in Sick Bay. Many asked if they could return to Earth. Although it would take only a year in space, forty years will have passed on Earth. So while it's possible, I don't think this is what any of you truly want."

A dismayed murmur broke out following his words.

Forty years? Her mother would be dead. Everyone she knew would be old.

Jan bit her lip to hold back the tears.

There would be no place for her or the rest of the Brides. Gary would have married someone else. No one would want her or need her.

"We need you," Delos concluded, "and we will cherish you as our wives, our dear partners. Brides, we'll leave you now to talk among yourselves. The oldest among you will act as the Brides' liaison to the Terilians." Turning his head, he gave Jan a significant look. "I'll meet with the Brides' liaison later."

Silently, Delos and the council filed out of the room. The women were left staring at each other. Many looked expectantly at Jan.

She needed to say the right thing. If she broke down, most of them would be sobbing in minutes.

Businesslike, that was it. "Okay, who's the oldest here?" Jan asked and called out her birthday. "Anyone older than that?"

No one was older than Jan's thirty-nine. As soon as that was determined, a thousand questions broke out. Waving her arms and raising her voice, Jan suggested that the women form a line and ask their questions. Later, she would share their questions with Delos.

A tall black woman spoke first. "Are we going to do what they want? Or are we going to resist?"

"How can we resist?" someone else called out.

The black woman glared fiercely. "Kill ourselves!"

"We need a lot more information before we make that decision," Jan said. *And I for one am not ready to die.*

"They messed with our bodies!" a young woman with curly brown hair exclaimed. "My sense of smell's on overdrive! Have they told us everything about this 'cellular overhaul'?"

The third woman in line spoke. "Ladies, where's your sense of adventure? A new planet? What a trip!"

A murmur of approval rolled through the Hall, indicating that a large number of the Brides agreed with her comment.

Wishing she had a notepad, Jan tried to memorize everyone's questions. Hours passed as almost everyone in the room spoke. What were the Terilians' bodies like?

"I'm not fucking some guy with a tail," one of the Brides called out.

"Yeah and I want to get a look at their cocks," someone else commented.

"If they even *have* cocks!" a third chimed in. Many of the women had been awakened the same way as Jan.

"It was wonderful!" one woman declared, blushing. "That's the first time I've ever had an orgasm."

The women asked about the Transition, the new planet and what "marriage" meant to the Terilians. And what was the Spring Running?

A young woman with short hair said, "I don't have a question. I just want to say that I had breast cancer back on Earth. Doctor Delos says it's gone now."

Another woman spoke eagerly. "He cured my diabetes too! No more insulin shots!"

So the aliens had done some good for them.

One of the women behind Jan began to sob.

Jan hesitated. *I don't know how to deal with people. I'm just a computer programmer, damn it.* Moving to the redhead, Jan awkwardly tried to comfort her by patting her shoulder. "I know it's hard," Jan said. "It's hard for everyone."

"But I was just about to get married!" The woman wiped tears with the back of her hand. "My wedding was all planned. I had the most beautiful white dress and…and the cake was ordered…and we'd put the deposit down for the band!"

"I know, honey, I'm in the same boat."

Another woman took over the comforting. "At least you were engaged," she told the redhead. "I never found a guy to marry. I worked as a wedding planner — but I never got to plan my own wedding!"

That gave Jan an idea. Perhaps she would mention it to Delos. A tiny shock of arousal went through her at the thought of him.

What's wrong with me? He's an alien!

The double doors slid open. Delos walked through with Taddus. The big primus touched the redhead's cheek. "Don't cry, pretty female. You'll soon have a husband who will love you dearly."

The redhead stared up at him, sniffing back her tears. Jan gazed at the young woman, startled. Was there desire in her eyes?

Jan's pulse quickened as Delos joined her. Why did his presence spark an instant awareness in her?

Perhaps because he'd been nearby when she experienced that superb orgasm. Her mind had somehow associated him with sexual pleasure. Maybe that was why she wanted to nestle closer to him. Close enough to feel his smooth skin rub against hers.

"Are you now the official liaison of the Brides?" he asked.

"Yes. Rigged that election, didn't you?"

"I knew you were the oldest," he said.

The impulse to touch him, to press her body against his, almost overwhelmed her.

His extraordinary blue eyes studied her face. "But I could have said, *Choose the wisest. Or the loveliest.* The result would have been the same."

Jan couldn't help herself. She took a step nearer. What would he do if she touched his hair?

Taddus gestured and the whistle for silence sounded. "Brides, I invite you to return to your cabins. You'll be called for another meeting in the Great Hall tomorrow. And let me just say how pleased and proud I am to have you all with us."

Jan thought, *Pompous ass.*

As the women left the Hall, Taddus came to Jan's side. "So you're the new liaison," he commented, taking her hand. He had a deep, dark odor that was faintly attractive but didn't stir her the same way Delos' scent did.

He raised her hand to his mouth and turned it palm upward. Was he going to kiss it?

His pink tongue darted out and he licked her palm. Jan gasped at the sensation, which reminded her of wet sandpaper. Despite herself, she trembled at the unusual feelings the gesture evoked within her.

The big male said, "Let me show you to your new cabin, my dear."

Delos took a step forward. "I believe that's *my* duty, Primus."

A low noise rumbled through the air. Jan blinked. Was the council member *growling* at the doctor?

The two males locked glances. Delos stood his ground.

"Go ahead, young Secondus," Taddus said at last. Turning back to Jan, his voice lowered. "Lovely One — be assured I'll find you at the Spring Running."

Solange Ayre

Chapter Three
ಸಾ

Jan's new quarters were small, eight by eight feet and seemed empty. Delos demonstrated the voice command that brought a computer console-table out of the wall. Drawers pulled out as well, containing several bright tunics. Another command and a large round bed opened above their heads. Jan frowned, wondering how she was supposed to get into it.

"Will I share this cabin with my husband, once I have one?"

Delos' eyes widened. "Live in the same room together, you mean? Of course not. People require privacy."

She tilted her head, looking at him. She kept picturing him naked on the bed, his eyes half-closed while she touched every inch of him. She'd never felt this way before—certainly not with Gary. "Why do I feel an irresistible urge to touch you?"

His startled eyes met hers for a moment, then he glanced away. "I thought you understood. The Transition has made you susceptible to Terilian male pheromones. All of us are exuding them to a great degree, this close to the Spring Running."

He was trying so hard to be scientific. Couldn't there be a simpler explanation—that she was attracted to him?

"But I didn't feel the urge when Taddus licked me." The memory gave her a nerve-jangling sensation unrelated to pleasure.

"What did you think of him?" She heard jealousy in his voice.

"Taddus made a speech. *You* spoke from your heart."

Delos seemed pleased. Gazing at him, she was distracted by the way the ends of his hair fell softly to his shoulders. "May I touch your hair?" *Your face, your body…*

"Go ahead."

As she drew near, the cocoa smell intensified. She wanted to rub her nipples against his chest. Lie beside him and entangle their legs.

She reached upward, running her palm down his hair. It was soft, like the fur of her tabby cat, back home. She wanted to stroke it again and again. She moved her hand slowly from the crown of his head all the way down, ending at his bare shoulder. Her palm caressed his shoulder and moved down his arm.

His eyes widened with apprehension and he took a step back. "When you touch me, I want to mate. Immediately."

"Why is that a problem? I thought we were brought here to become wives to males like you."

He turned away, breathing hard. The spicy odor in the room increased. She knew, with her newly enhanced senses, that he was struggling with intense desire.

"Yes." He spoke with difficulty. "But we swore—all of us—that no one would have intercourse until the Spring Running."

Disappointment shot through her, even as the impulse to touch him increased. She desperately needed to think about something else.

She looked around, searching for a more neutral subject. "How am I supposed to reach the bed?"

"Most of us like our beds near the ceiling. But you probably can't jump that high yet."

Before she realized what he intended, he scooped her into his arms. She shivered at the sudden intimacy, even as she wondered how a slender male like him could lift her so effortlessly. He crouched, then sprang into the air. In another moment, she was lying on the bed, Delos beside her.

Her heart raced from the leap. Even more disturbing was his proximity. She had to keep fighting the need to stroke her palms over his body.

"Can you all leap like that?" she asked.

"Yes. And you will too, once the cellular uptake is complete."

Jan raised her eyebrows. Now that she'd lived through it, she realized she'd enjoyed the sensational leap through the air.

There was a downside, though. Suppose the Brides decided to resist? If they eventually convinced the Terilians to take them back to Earth, they'd be freaks.

Her mind shying away from the disturbing thought, she bounced lightly on the bed. Unlike the hard hospital bed, this mattress felt malleable, almost as though there was jelly under the woven cover.

What would he do if she parted her thighs and stroked herself? Would he be shocked, or would he watch eagerly? She wondered why she felt such a strange need to tease him, to provoke him.

She'd better start working through the Brides' list of questions. "We're all curious about what you males look like naked."

His brow creased. "We're much like humans."

"Have you seen any of the Brides without clothing?" *Not that our tunics conceal much.*

"That's different—I'm a doctor."

"Well then, doctor, you shouldn't be embarrassed about bodies." She didn't want to reveal how interested she was in seeing his most private features, so she threw a challenge into her voice. "Or are you afraid to reveal what Terilian male anatomy looks like?"

Raising his chin, he knelt facing her and lifted his tunic over his head. Although Delos was slender, his body was muscular, from his shoulders and sculpted biceps to his firm abdomen and tapered waist.

"Your muscles are well developed." She fought the urge to run her hands over his contours. What would he do if she caressed his smooth chest? Licked his dark nipples? "How do you maintain that physique in space?"

"We're required to log in five hours of exercise out of every forty. Life will be difficult on our new planet for the first few years. It's essential to maintain our physical strength."

He turned. A two-inch width of fur, brown like his hair with variegated tawny spots, ran down the middle of his back and disappeared into his tights.

"Is that fur what you call your 'pelt'?" she asked.

"That's right." Remaining with his back to her, he raised up on his knees and pulled down his tights. His slightly rounded buttocks were firm and taut. The fur narrowed, ending at the crack of his ass.

No tail. Aside from his line of fur, his backside looked much like a human man's. One with a particularly attractive butt. She drew a quick breath as she imagined herself caressing those muscular cheeks.

He discarded his tights and turned. Her eyes were drawn to his cock, which stood long and straight against his stomach, much darker than his pale brown skin.

Instantly, her pussy went wet at the sight.

She stared at the head of his cock. Instead of the familiar mushroom-shape of humans, his cock had a long, cylindrical head that extended several inches back.

She strove for a detached tone. "I assume you're sexually aroused right now?"

"Yes. Most of us struggle with constant arousal, this close to the Spring Running." His tone, precise and scientific, was belied by his huge erection. Like her, he was trying to sound detached but Jan wasn't fooled.

"Isn't it painful to walk around like that?"

"It's been two years since our females died. Terilians weren't meant to go without mating for so long. The drugs help but only temporarily." He moved closer on the bed and put his hands on her shoulders. She shivered at his sensual touch. "And when I'm with you, your presence overrides the drugs."

She couldn't take her eyes off that fascinating cock. She wanted to touch it, feel the skin under her palm. Lick him and taste him as though she were starving and he was her first meal in days.

Delos moved his palms in circles, leaving a trail of tingling wildfire wherever he touched. Gary's hands had never thrilled her like this. Never before had she felt such intense desire, such a desperate need for coupling that transcended all common sense.

"I could spend days touching you," he said, his voice suddenly husky.

She forced herself to speak, when all she wanted to do was throw her head back and drink in his caresses. "Tell me about the Spring Running. The Brides are curious."

He frowned, momentarily pressing his hand to her lips. She was tempted to kiss his hand and suck his fingers into her mouth.

"I'm forbidden to speak of it. You'll be told what to do on the day itself."

She persisted, "But what happens that day will pair off Brides and husbands?"

"Yes."

"If you can—will you choose me?"

He wrapped his arms around her, drawing her against his chest. She sighed and put her arms around his waist. Somehow she'd known this was coming. And now that it had, it felt completely right.

His voice lowered. "My sole desire is to find you that day, then mate with you over and over until you scream with the pleasure I give you."

Arousal washed over her at his words. "And if that happens, does that make me your wife?" She pulled back, looking up into his face.

Sorrow darkened his expression and she turned cold inside.

"Taddus marked you for his own today. He will claim you as his Bride, don't doubt it. I'm a secondus, he is a primus. I must yield to him."

"And I have no choice in the matter?"

"That's not our way."

"Then how is that different from rape?" Jan demanded.

"Because on that day, your body won't resist him. During the Spring Running, our bodies crave sex the way our lungs crave air. He'll mate with you and you'll find great pleasure in it." Jan sensed that Delos was telling the truth but he looked down as though the words pained him.

"You can't know that for sure," she argued. "Maybe that's how it works with your females. But I'm from Earth. And if I don't like a guy, I don't mate with him. I kick him to the curb."

"The genetic overhaul is making you more like our females every day. Don't you have a saying on Earth, 'biology is destiny'?"

"Not in modern times it isn't," she retorted.

He frowned. "Are you always this sarcastic? Our females never spoke like this."

"Too bad you didn't kidnap some other species."

For a moment their gazes locked. Then Delos' mouth quirked up in a smile. "No, I'm happy with the way things worked out. Earth females are fascinating creatures. We're all counting the days until the Spring Running."

Jan took a deep breath. It didn't help to clear her head. His proximity made her feel dizzy and intoxicated. The longer he sat close to her, the more her arousal increased. Tempted to grasp him around the waist and pull him down on top of her, she dug her nails into her palm.

Don't get carried away. He's an alien and a kidnapper. Even if he says they had to do it, even if you like him, what they did was wrong.

If you have to, let him give you pleasure. But don't get emotionally involved.

"The Brides have questions about what you Terilians are like when you mate. You said intercourse is forbidden. But on Earth, we do many things to please each other aside from intercourse."

He gently cupped the side of her face. "I could talk about these matters for hours. But I'd rather show you." He gazed into her eyes, waiting for her answer.

"Then show me." Her voice shook with fear and anticipation.

"Lie on your back. If you think you'll enjoy it, I'll demonstrate a loving pleasure that husbands do for their wives."

Trembling, Jan stretched out on the bed. *I'm the guinea pig here. I'm going to let this stranger touch my body. He's not even a human man. He's an alien.*

And I can hardly wait.

Every breath flooded her with the scent of him, a scent that made her nipples tighten and her pussy swell with arousal. But she didn't want him to know. She didn't want to give him that much power over her.

With a mocking note in her voice, she said, "I guess you people don't believe in pillows."

Delos smiled. "Bed!" he commanded. "Make a pillow. And incline the female's back at a twenty degree angle."

The bed shifted, the mattress forming up underneath her so that her back was raised and a "pillow" form elevated her head.

"Much better." She licked her lips. Her heart pounded.

He leaned over her, passion blazing in those pale-blue eyes. "What have you done to me, Janis?" His voice was husky with emotion. "No matter how hard I try, I can't stop thinking about you. Even my dreams are filled with your scent."

"It's just biology, Delos."

"You think so?"

"You said it yourself."

He brought his face closer. She wondered if he would kiss her but instead he rubbed his cheek against hers. His scent filled her nostrils. She gasped as her pussy throbbed with sudden, desperate need.

His hand stroked slowly through her hair.

"Your ears are unusual," he murmured. "So funny and round and hairless." He took her right earlobe in his mouth and ran his tongue over it. Her stomach quivered as she enjoyed the slightly wet roughness. It wasn't enough to hurt but enough to provide a pleasurable contrast as he sucked on her earlobe and then licked around the whorl of her ear. She threw her head back, breathing hard, positioning herself to give him easy access. She'd had lovers who'd kissed her ear before—she'd always adored the sensation—but no one had ever taken such leisurely time to lick, to suck, to taste.

He brushed her hair back from her face, his fingers tangling in the long strands. "Black hair like yours is highly prized by us. It's partly what makes you so very beautiful."

Would she ever have the nerve to tell him she wasn't considered beautiful on Earth?

He buried his face against her chin and again his tongue caressed her as he licked his way down her neck. His tongue was soft and slow, taking long licks as though he savored a particularly delectable dessert. She closed her eyes in enjoyment, stretching her neck. A soft "Oh!" escaped her as he explored her right shoulder with his warm mouth and tongue. His hands moved sensually down her back.

She wanted to lie there for hours, melting under his fingers, thrilling to the gentle, teasing scrape of his tongue on her sensitized skin.

He switched to captivating soft nibbles, letting her feel just a hint of his teeth. Her pussy felt heavy, slick with liquid. Would he touch her there?

He'd talked about demonstrating loving pleasure. What did that mean to a Terilian? Did their females have orgasms like human women? Would he continue licking her until she expired from unfulfilled arousal? Or would he satisfy her?

Suppose she did something that shocked him or offended him. Something taboo.

"Janis—is something wrong?"

"I don't know what's expected, what's permitted."

He gazed into her eyes. The expression on his face was serious and concerned. "Don't worry. I've learned a great deal about human sexuality. Terilians and humans, we're much alike."

That was reassuring. And so far, everything he'd done had made her shudder with delight.

She wanted more—more licking, more touching. She wanted that lovely sandpaper tongue on her breasts.

He flicked the nape of her neck. She moaned.

"Am I pleasing you?" he asked.

"Yes!" She stared up at him, enjoying the dreamy, lust-filled expression on his face. "What about you?"

"When the plan was first proposed, I never imagined finding a female who smelled and tasted so wonderful. How will I ever bear to leave your bed?"

She didn't want to think about it either. "Let's just enjoy the moment." She touched his cheek, watching his eyes half-close in satisfaction.

She knew what she wanted and she was going to ask for it. He'd implied he wouldn't be offended. *So let's put it to the test.*

"Delos? Did your females have breasts like Earth women?"

"Yes but not so round."

"Did they like to be touched there?"

"With permission. Are you granting that to me?"

"Oh, yes." She arched her back and lifted her tunic.

Chapter Four

୬

Weeks ago, Delos had brain-linked with the ship's computer and absorbed millions of words uplinked from Earth computers about human anatomy. Intellectually, he knew what would sexually stimulate Janis. But would she really respond to a nonhuman?

He'd realized a year ago that his people wouldn't survive the journey without wives. After he'd made his report, the astrogation team went into overdrive, searching for planets with females who could fulfill the need to mate.

They'd all wanted to survive, to save their lives. They hadn't expected more than that.

They'd never thought to find enticing females who would stir their very souls.

Delos gazed down at the achingly beautiful human, entranced by her soft white globes tipped with dark pink circles. While he'd seen many of the Brides naked, it was one thing to treat them professionally, quite another to lie beside his chosen one in bed.

He'd been longing to touch her breasts, feel their softness, stroke those enticing nipples. But he'd held back, not wanting to startle her.

Now she'd told him she *wanted* his touch. Excitement raced through him.

He took her right breast in his hand, caressing the nipple with his thumb. She murmured deep in her throat and his organ stirred.

He slid down on the bed. Still toying with her right breast, he took her left breast in his mouth, savoring the warm, slightly salty taste of her skin. Flicking the tip of her nipple with his tongue, he growled with satisfaction. She gave out a little cry that excited him beyond bearing. He licked her nipple again while his thumb and forefinger rolled her other nipple between them.

"Yes. That's good," she gasped.

He closed his lips over her left breast and sucked, drawing her nipple into his mouth. It was hotter than the rest of her flesh and as he licked and teased, the tender flesh grew and lengthened. He raised his head, fascinated by the way it had doubled in size in a few moments. Her engorged nipple was as deeply pink as the berries on a *jorem* plant—and tastier.

"Are all human females as responsive as you?" he asked.

She stared back at him for a long moment. Confusion crossed her face. "I've always enjoyed sex…but I've never felt this way before." Her fingers slid into his hair, caressing his scalp. "You're not going to do this with anyone else?"

"Don't worry about that," he said fervently. He had the distinct feeling she'd already spoiled him for any other female. Enticing as some of the other Brides had seemed at first, now he knew he'd found his true mate.

And that would be a problem, if Taddus claimed her. *When* Taddus claimed her.

He didn't want to think about the big primus now. His only aim was to give Janis such pleasure that she'd never forget him.

He licked the soft skin between her breasts. "Don't stop," she gasped. She stroked his neck and shoulder, her fingers trailing desire wherever she touched. He shivered.

Remember your vow. No one mates until the Spring Running.

But he couldn't help imagining how it would ease him to plunge his throbbing penis into her slick channel.

This is for her tonight, not for you. But he'd never wanted to mate so badly before. Doubt shook him. Could he keep his vow?

He wanted to caress her female pelt until she parted her legs. He'd breathe deeply, inhaling more of her fragrant arousal. Then he'd rub the head of his organ against her labia. Would she moan? Beg him to mate with her? Nothing would feel better than that first hard, hot thrust.

Stop thinking about mounting her. Concentrate on pleasing her.

"Do you enjoy it when I suck your nipples?"

"Yes, Delos — more!"

He put his arm around her shoulders and turned her toward him. The bed shifted slightly to brace her in this new position. He closed his lips over her right breast, already swollen from the caress of his fingers and sucked hard. Her breathing changed.

She moved her hips restlessly. "Delos. Touch me."

He looked up from the tender flesh of her nipple long enough to give her a curious look. Wasn't that what he was doing?

She steered his fingers to her female pelt. He was eager to caress that part of her. Terilian females had a small curve of fur surrounding their sex that matched their back pelt. Janis' pelt was unique, a riot of tiny curls that matched the black hair on her head. He ran his fingers slowly through her curls, rewarded by her moan of approval.

She raised her knees and parted her legs. Exactly as he'd imagined. The intoxicating aroma of her arousal thrilled him. He desperately wanted to bury his face in her sex, breathe deeply, lap the sweet cream that was already flowing from her.

Not too fast, Del. Don't frighten her.

What beautiful legs she had…rounded knees, plump thighs. He stroked them, seduced by the softness of her skin. She whimpered as his hands moved upward, his fingers teasing the creases between her thighs and vagina.

Much like her nipples, her labia were bright pink and swollen — eager for his touch. Tentatively he brushed his hand lightly against her sex. She moaned, raising her hips wantonly as though begging to be mounted.

He caressed her slowly, his hand moving in a gentle rhythm that soon had her arching toward him with every stroke. Enjoying the hot wetness that drenched his fingers, he raised his hand to his mouth to savor the fascinating taste of her.

The words broke from his throat. "I wish I could mate with you."

Her fingers closed around the head of his erect organ. Growling with startled delight, he moved against her hand, knowing he couldn't achieve release from a caress but unable to stop himself. Her firm touch was both a delight and a torment. If only he could take her now. He'd give her a mounting she'd never forget—plunge his engorged organ into her over and over, a wild, passionate mating. The memory of it would flood her mind whenever she saw him or inhaled his scent.

But he knew what would happen to him if he broke his vow. The thought cooled him long enough to gently remove her hand.

"This is just for you," he said. "Let me give you pleasure."

"But you look like *you're* all ready."

"I've been ready for weeks." Ever since she'd appeared on the transport slab, her mass of black hair stark against her white garment, he'd ached for her. He remembered the way her dark eyelashes lay against her pink skin, her round breasts half-revealed by the low neckline of her garment. In the middle of directing his orderlies, he'd stopped and thought, *Mine*.

Her voice came low. "Are you sure we can't have sex?"

Surprise mingled with triumph. She *wanted* to mate with him.

"Not until the Spring Running." He leaned forward and rubbed his cheek against hers, marking her with his scent. "Beautiful Janis. Let me give you an orgasm."

"Yes. Keep touching me…"

He knew where the female human pleasure center resided—high above the vaginal opening, in the single clitoris. Quite unlike Terilian females, who had two. Conversely, many females didn't like being touched there directly.

He touched her vagina, stroking lightly, fondling the hot, wet opening. Watching her reaction closely, he smiled when she shifted on the bed, parting her legs farther. He continued his caresses, letting the back of his hand brush lightly against her clitoris with every stroke.

Her lovely sex was open and glistening. Inviting his organ inside. If only he were allowed, now would be the time to thrust inside her.

Would it be too much temptation to rub the head of his penis against her?

Don't do it, Del. You'll never be able to stop.

Instead he parted her labia, entering her with the tip of his finger.

She thrust her hips, trying to take more of his finger inside. He withdrew.

"Lie still," he ordered. He lowered his head and licked her navel, feeling her tremble. Holding her hips firmly in his hands, he laved his tongue over her stomach. She whimpered with need.

He cupped her mound in his hand, enjoying her heat, which increased even more when he squeezed lightly.

"Delos, stop teasing me." Her voice was edgy, ragged. "Really, I can't take any more!"

She was his now, his female. She lay open to him, awaiting pleasure.

Exquisitely slowly, he entered her with one finger, feeling her wet folds give way before his invasion. Throwing her head back, she let out a cry. He pushed in farther, sighing with satisfaction when her inner muscles clenched around his finger.

Leaning closer, he whispered, "Is that what you want?"

She gasped, "Yes! More!"

He drew his finger in and out, wishing it were his organ that traveled back and forth in her clinging pink channel, stroking and milking him.

"Delos! Please!"

He added another finger and moved his hand faster. Her cries increased, a frantic note in her voice. She stared up at the ceiling, panting, jerking her hips every time his fingers plunged inside. He gazed down at her, fascinated with the enraptured expression on her face.

Her cheeks were flushed, her lips pink and parted. She'd never seemed more beautiful. His eyes went out of focus as he imagined the day of the Spring Running. Her delighted cries at his powerful thrusts...the way she would spur him on, begging to be mounted again and again...

"Oh! So good!"

"Come for me, beautiful one. Take your pleasure." He thrust deep with his fingers. She wriggled hard against his hand while he rubbed his thumb against her swollen clitoris. She screamed and her vagina spasmed. Groaning triumphantly, he felt her strong muscles pulse around his hand over and over.

When the day came and he mounted her at last, she would give him his full release. He was sure of it. And his organ would provide her with the greatest joy she had ever known.

He thrust more slowly now. He still felt her opening and closing around his fingers but less frequently, less strongly. He moved his hand against her wetness and took her breast in his mouth, nibbling her erect nipple. Trembling, shaking, she pulsed around his fingers again.

At last she lay still. She turned her head and looked at him. "Delos. That was wonderful."

"That was just the beginning. At the Spring Running, I'll take you over and over, give you orgasm after orgasm, until you barely remember your own name."

Her eyes widened.

Withdrawing his hand, he gathered her against his chest, his chin resting on the top of her head. She was so soft, so warm. Her hand stole into his and held it. He felt his heart turn over in his chest.

Mine.

Until Taddus claims her.

No. Mine.

She stirred. "Delos? Is something wrong?"

He tightened his hold. "Nothing's wrong. Sleep now."

She yawned. "Will you sleep too?"

Hesitating, he said, "I'll stay if you wish." His wife had been very private, even for a Terilian, never wanting to share the bed after mating. He wasn't used to sleeping beside a female.

"Stay if you *want* to stay," she shot back.

He had no desire to leave her. And he knew as soon as he returned to his own cabin, the council would contact him, demanding a report. Had Janis Stone been receptive? In his opinion, would the human females accept their mates at the Spring Running? Most importantly, would they orgasm strongly enough to draw release from the males?

Let them wait. "I'll stay," he whispered, closing his eyes.

Their survival depended on his answers. But at this moment, all he cared about was Janis. And all he could think about was how much he wanted to keep her for his own.

One Thousand Brides

* * * * *

Jan woke with the feeling that hours had passed. Delos was still with her, turned on his side facing her. His eyelids twitched as he dreamed.

How strange that she'd been able to fall into a restful sleep beside this alien male. That she'd let him touch her pussy, fuck her with his skillful fingers. That he'd said, *Come for me* and she had.

He was everything she'd found lacking in Gary. Handsome to look at. Strong and gentle at the same time. With hands and a mouth that felt magical on her skin.

Drawing nearer, she kissed him. He sighed but didn't wake. She kissed him again, darting her tongue between his lips.

He rolled onto his back. His eyes flew open and focused on her. "What did you do to my mouth?" he demanded.

She smiled. "I kissed you. Don't Terilians kiss?"

"No. Mouth to skin is normal. Mouth to mouth seems very strange."

Jan raised her brows. "This shouldn't be a one-way street. Everything can't be the Terilian way."

"But ours is the advanced culture."

"Now you sound like Taddus."

"I apologize," he said instantly.

She propped herself on one elbow, gazing down into his beautiful, pale blue eyes. Breathing deeply, she took in his scent. All she wanted was to feel his sensual hands on her again.

What was wrong with her? She had to stay in control here. She had a duty to the rest of the Brides.

"Listen, Delos. Many times on Earth, two different cultures have come together. Not always successfully. When it works, it's because both cultures are willing to be…flexible. Learn from each other."

"I don't know what the other males will think."

"The Brides will like it."

He reached up, pulling her closer. "All right. Teach me how to kiss."

A tiny flame glowed inside her. He'd listened to her.

"I'll press my lips to yours and you press back. Then we'll open our mouths and let our tongues stroke each other."

The crease in his brow revealed this troubled him. But when she put her mouth over his, caressing his lips lightly, he responded, moving his mouth under hers.

Then she drew her tongue across his and he jerked, startled. She persisted, exploring the sweet cave of his mouth, running her tongue over his teeth. His curved fangs made kissing him a unique experience.

Caressing the side of his face, she slid her tongue in and out of his mouth. She was thrilled when he did the same. Their tongues dodged and encountered, glided and teased.

He flipped them so that she was lying on her back and he was above her. Kneeling between her thighs, he lowered his head and took her mouth, thrusting his tongue almost as though it were his cock.

Jan's breathing quickened. "You learn fast."

"I've absorbed much information about human ways. It only comes to mind when I need it." He kissed her again, thoroughly exploring her mouth, then sucking on her tongue. Jan shifted her hips restlessly.

"That arouses you?" he asked.

She couldn't deny it. Her pussy was wet and throbbing. "Yes. Do you like kissing?"

"It's unusual, but I think I do. Almost as much as I like licking you all over." Slowly he moved down her body, licking and sucking her skin. He spent a long time teasing her nipples, rolling and flicking them with his tongue, then soothing them with gentle sucking. An ache of wanting spread through her pussy. Every time his mouth touched her breasts, she felt flames lick her core.

He moved down, his tongue darting into her navel. Ripples of pleasure spread through her. Her nipples tingled and burned where his rough tongue had touched them. Her hot channel yearned to be filled with his big cock.

"Ready for more pleasure?" he murmured.

"Yes," she groaned in reply. "Please, Delos."

He spread her thighs apart, caressing the soft skin with his hands, then buried his face in her pussy. Suddenly panicked, she asked, "What are you going to do?"

"Lick you until you have an orgasm."

She shivered, excited by his words. But she couldn't help asking, "Are you sure you know what you're doing?"

He opened her labia with his thumbs. "Oh, I think so." She smiled at the confidence in his voice. He lowered his head again and gave her a long lick all the way up her labia to her clit. She gasped and opened her legs farther as he did the same on the other side.

Yes, he knows exactly what he's doing.

Wetness leaked from her hot, swollen channel as his tongue darted and danced over her pussy, teasing the opening, then lingering on her clit just long enough to make her crave more.

As each touch of his tongue thrilled her, she felt herself opening to him, anticipating the next contact. There was nothing else like this. Delos was doing it exactly right, exactly the way she liked and she wanted it to last forever. Every stroke of his tongue was heavenly.

She'd never been so wet in her life, never needed an orgasm so intensely. She raised her hips, trying to get more of his wonderful mouth, his pleasure-giving tongue.

He swirled around her clit and she cried out, arching up. She would have pleaded for more but she'd forgotten how to speak. She wanted to stay like this, hovering on the brink of coming, experiencing shudders of delight every time he licked her.

His mouth fastened over her clit, sucking it gently. At the same moment, he entered her hot, swollen channel with his thumb. The two sensations at once overwhelmed her, pushing her into strong spasms of incredible pleasure. Her hips bucked against his mouth. He growled deep in his throat, then his tongue swirled over her clit again and again as he fucked her with his thumb. Waves of delight rolled through her. She thrashed against him, unable to control herself, unable to stop the high keening issuing from her throat.

She drew deep breaths as her orgasm slowly receded. Finally she lowered her knees, still feeling the pulsing, ebbing waves. He moved to lie at her side, stroking her breasts.

"I've never felt this way before," Delos said. "If I were your husband, I'd do that for you every day. Sometimes I'd give you an orgasm that way and other times I'd make you wait until I mounted you."

Typical male exaggeration. "I'm sure you wouldn't want to do it *every* day."

His brows rose in surprise. "Of course I would. Nothing's more healthy. We have a saying, 'An orgasm a day keeps the doctor away'."

She put her arms around his waist. "But I don't want to keep the doctor away. I want to keep the doctor close." This near to him, she was very aware of his erect cock against her body. "Delos? Let me do something for you now." Tentatively, she stroked his long shaft.

He gazed at her, a crease between his brows. "I can't achieve release like that." He lifted her hand away from him. "Females are lucky—they can seek pleasure so many different ways. But for males, there is one method only. His mate's orgasmic contractions trigger the male's release."

Jan drew in a quick breath, awestruck. No wonder Delos was so skilled in bed.

Among the Terilians, there'd never be a male who'd take his pleasure and then roll over and go to sleep, leaving his wife unsatisfied.

"You can't even masturbate?"

"Females can. Males cannot." His voice was rueful. "Thus our dilemma. Do you see why we need you so badly? Not only for offspring, for companionship, for your lovely softness." Lying against him, she felt him take a deep breath. "Terilians can no more survive without sex than humans can live without food. Without the release of mating, we'll die."

"Don't talk about dying," she whispered.

He stroked her body slowly, not in a sexual way now but lovingly. As though he cared about her. The way she'd come to care for him.

Damn it, Jan! What a fool you are. Delos says the primus will claim you. Why fall for someone you can't have?

How could she help it? Delos was so caring, so handsome, so sexually pleasing.

To distract herself, she asked questions about Terilian culture, about the planet they would colonize, about what marriage meant to the males on the ship. He answered in detail and, she thought, frankly and openly.

Finally he asked a question of his own. "Do you think the Brides will resist? Or will they agree to be our wives?"

She sighed. She'd been thinking about this and hadn't yet reached a conclusion. "I don't know."

"What do you feel, in your own heart? Do you want to return to Earth?"

"Forty years later? When most of the people I knew will be gone?" She shook her head. "No, I have no desire to go back. Especially since you and the other doctors changed us. If we went back to Earth, we'd be different from all other women. That was wrong, Delos. You should have asked our permission."

"The council made that decision. And it's to your benefit. I truly think you'll enjoy having claws."

Chapter Five

༃

Jan pulled out of his arms and sat upright on the bed. "What are you talking about? Taddus never mentioned *claws*."

Delos sat up too. "Humans are weak and defenseless. We thought you'd better have weapons like the rest of us, especially when facing life on the new planet." He raised his eyebrows. "From what I understand, there's a lot of crime on Earth. Pretend I'm a criminal coming at you." He growled and lunged at her.

Instinctively she raised her hands up, going for his eyes. Inch-long claws shot out from underneath her fingernails. Jan gasped.

Delos caught her wrists in his hands. She stared into his eyes and he released her.

She brought her hands up to her face. Her fingers shook as she gazed at these new additions to her body.

"How do I put them away?" Her voice quavered.

"They'll retract once your body understands you don't need them right now."

Claws. It seemed so odd to suddenly have claws.

"Did you notice the rough strips of material on the doorway?" he asked. "You can sharpen your claws there. Always keep them sharp. Dull claws are slovenly."

Her claws had a pearly sheen. Perhaps they were rather…attractive.

And she could see how they might be useful. "Show me yours, Delos."

He held up his hands. As fast as ten switchblades, his claws extended—two inches long, shiny and as spotlessly clean and sharp as surgical knives.

Her brows rose. "Wow. And I let you touch me with those hands?"

Noiselessly, his claws retracted. "Janis!" He pulled her into his embrace. "A sane male *can't* hurt a female with his claws. It's one of our strongest taboos. If a male goes feral and hurts a female, all other males hunt him down and kill him."

"That's good to hear—I guess. Does it happen often?"

"No. Much less often than on Earth." He stroked her skin soothingly. "I know how frequently 'domestic violence' is a problem among humans. It's extremely rare among Terilians. Tell the Brides—perhaps it will help reconcile them to their new destinies."

She tilted her head. "Delos, I thought of something else—another way to help everyone adjust. After the Spring Running, when everyone pairs up? Is there some kind of ceremony to mark the occasion?"

"A ceremony?" He didn't seem to know what she meant. "Mated couples return in pairs, bound to each other by scent and cord. Why would a ceremony be necessary?"

She gave him an exasperated look. "What did I say earlier about sharing our cultures? I have a way to make all this more palatable for the Brides."

* * * * *

The next day, Jan and all the other women were served First Meal in the Great Hall. The Brides were given a ship's schedule, which Jan studied with some surprise. The Terilian days were long—twenty-eight hours of seventy-two minutes each—but they were broken into more meals and sleep-times than human days.

Days were divided into six meals, two nap periods and two work periods. However, Terilians were required to work only four days out of each eight-day week. Jan wondered if this would be the standard operating procedure when they arrived at the new planet, which would presumably require a heavier work schedule.

After they ate delicious yellow berries and drank a spicy hot beverage, Jan rose and spoke to the other women, telling them everything she'd learned from Delos.

"Marriage is a committed pair-bonding until the next Spring Running. If we mate with them, most of us will have babies by the time we land on the new planet. Three or four babies, actually, because Terilian females conceive in multiples and so will we."

Many of the women in the room looked horrified. Jan continued, "But Terilian young grow up much faster than human children. By the age of six months, they're talking and dressing themselves. By the age of twelve, they're teenagers, learning their professions. Secondus Delos is only twenty-eight years old but he's been a doctor for the last ten years."

"Don't they have birth control?" a dark-haired woman demanded.

Jan wrinkled her brow, wishing she'd been able to make a PowerPoint presentation. This was a lot for everyone to take in.

"Husbands and wives can mate whenever they want—just like humans—but wives don't get pregnant while they have children to tend. When the children reach the age of twelve and leave to learn their professions, another Spring Running is held. At that time, mated couples can stay together—or choose new mates. And the wives will conceive again."

She went on to tell them about Terilian male anatomy.

The other women were still waiting expectantly. *I have to tell them everything. They must have all the facts.*

She'd been a computer programmer. A solitary one who'd had few boyfriends until Gary. She wasn't used to speaking of intimate details.

This is different. You're their liaison. Tell them what it was like with Delos.

The Hall was utterly hushed as she spoke about what they'd done together in bed.

Beth, the redheaded woman who had cried at the first meeting, addressed Jan when she finished. "So the doctor is nice. Maybe the rest of them are brutes!"

Jan explained how the males couldn't achieve orgasm without a female. "I think—I think if we mate with them, we'll enjoy it." *The rest of you will, anyway.*

If only she could be Delos' wife. But it seemed that if Taddus wanted her, he had first choice.

It wasn't fair. All her life she'd wanted to be beautiful. In this culture she was but it was working against her.

The women seemed interested.

"I get to come first? Always?"

"They can't jack off?"

"You *sure* they don't have tails?"

Jan answered everything she could. Finally, Beth spoke again. "I don't care! They made me miss my wedding! Now I'll never have one!"

Jan drew a deep breath. "Secondus Delos thinks we can do something about that."

* * * * *

"The Brides want *what*?" Primus Taddus demanded.

"They want a ceremony to celebrate the marriages." Raising his brows, Delos added, "And if you ever want to be happily mated, Primus, I think we'd better do what they want."

Primus Asher linked with the handheld computer Delos had given him, then passed it to Primus Goldus. "But Delos! How can we grow flowers in time? And we don't have any horses on shipboard!"

Goldus chimed in worriedly, "There are no children aboard to carry a ring on a pillow. And I don't understand this part about *garters*."

"I downloaded samples from many different human cultures," Delos said quickly. "I don't think the details are important. The Brides expect festivities. Music—and a feast."

"Ridiculous," snorted Primus Bardus. "You want us to put all these resources into a *party*? Look at this estimate for computer time!"

"I want us to put our resources into *making our Brides happy*," Delos retorted. "Let me remind you, if they resist us, we won't have a good Spring Running."

"How can they resist our pheromones?" Asher asked.

"The human females are strong-minded," Delos answered. "If they decide to resist, I can't guarantee a happy outcome, pheromones or not."

"Why should we give these primitives the upper hand?"

"True, their culture is not as advanced as ours. But the human females are little different from Terilian females." Sighing inwardly, Delos wondered why they were refusing to see what he realized so clearly. "You've all been married. I've been married. Did it ever do us any good to oppose something our wives really wanted?"

All fell silent. Asher grimaced down at the handheld computer. Bardus cleared his throat. Goldus rolled his eyes.

Finally, Hirdos said, "Well…perhaps you know best. I vote for the ceremony."

Eventually the vote came down to four to one, with only Taddus voting against the others. Delos could hardly wait to tell Janis that her plan would be followed.

"A moment of your time," Taddus said as the other council members departed. The big primus held up his right hand and extended his claws. "You're going to Janis now, aren't you?"

"I need to tell her about the council's decision."

Taddus took him by the shoulder. Delos stood rooted, trying to ignore the pain as long claws bit into his flesh.

"I can't stop you from mounting her at the Spring Running. But don't forget whose mate she'll be."

Delos stared into Taddus' yellow eyes. "You can claim her. But you'll never have her heart."

"You're naïve, young Secondus. Females love males with power."

"Janis isn't like that!"

"She'll forget all about you once I've taken her a few dozen times." Taddus brought his face closer. "Is she as ripe and juicy as she looks? Have you licked the sweet cream from her sex?"

Sweat trickled down Delos' face from the pain in his shoulder. He trembled with the effort of controlling himself. Losing the battle, he extended his claws.

"Will you raise your claws to me?" Taddus whispered. "You know our law."

Gritting his teeth, Delos forced his claws back inside.

"I didn't *think* you wanted to be gelded by the council." Taddus rubbed his cheek against Delos'. A growl escaped Delos at the insult.

Taddus smirked. "Go to her now, with my scent on you." Laughing, he left the council chamber.

* * * * *

Delos found Janis in the Great Hall, sharing Third Meal with the rest of the Brides. He located a free stool and pulled it up beside her.

"Afternoon greetings, Dr. Delos," she said coolly, as if they were mere acquaintances. As though she'd never writhed under his mouth in the throes of an orgasm.

"The same to you, Janis Stone," he answered with formal politeness, longing to do something that would establish her as his own in front of everyone present.

He gave the rest of the Brides a general smile. Many of them had been his patients and would be again, once they conceived. He couldn't help noticing that some gave him covertly interested glances and he wondered what Janis had been saying about him.

Did a male ever know what females discussed when no males were present?

The Brides had been served a great delicacy—*tregarth* shoots—but apparently no one had demonstrated how to eat them. They were chewing on the hard ends of the stalks, which were edible but bitter.

"Is there some trick to eating these?" Jan asked him.

He showed her how to hold the stalk in her left palm, extend the claw on her right forefinger and run the sharp edge along the stalk to release the thick white cream within.

"Scoop it out with your finger."

She gave him a doubtful look but did as he'd instructed, lifting a dollop of cream to her mouth and licking it. Her face changed. "That's delicious!"

The other Brides were eager to experiment. Soon they were opening the stalks, some successfully, some awkwardly.

Cutting too deeply brought great gobs of the cream dripping out, provoking little shrieks from Brides with stained tunics.

"Are you hungry?" Jan asked him.

Only for you. "I had Second Meal," he said, not really an answer.

Looking into his eyes, she skimmed her finger through the cream, then held it to his lips. "Have some."

His gaze never left hers as he grasped her wrist and sucked her finger slowly into his mouth. The oozing sweetness invaded his senses, along with the wonderful taste of Janis' skin. His tongue laved her long finger, his lips caressing her flesh. He teased the juncture between her second and third fingers with short, quick strokes. She gave him a wide-eyed look and repossessed her finger.

He wanted to talk to her apart from all the other Brides. "Would you like to see more of the ship?"

She agreed to that and they left together. As soon as they reached the corridor, she turned to him. "Did you speak to the council about the marriage ceremony?"

"Yes." He couldn't wait to touch her. He put his hands on her shoulders. "Give me a kiss first, then I'll tell you what they said."

She smiled. "They must have agreed to my plan. You wouldn't tease me if it were bad news." She raised her face and parted her lips.

The sweetness of their kiss almost broke his heart. *Taddus will never kiss her like this.* He recalled how he'd told the council about this fascinating pre-mating technique. Taddus had sneered and declared it perverted.

The primus will never understand her. He'll mate with her but he won't care about her the way I do.

His tongue stroked hers as their lips melded together. The kiss turned more sensual, more urgent. Heat built in his loins when he felt her breasts pressing into him.

"Now tell me," she demanded when their lips finally parted.

For a moment he couldn't remember what they'd been talking about. All he wanted was to take her into a cabin—any cabin—and mate with her. Or, since that wasn't possible, pleasure her again with his hands and mouth.

"The marriage ceremony?" she reminded him.

"Oh, yes—the ceremony. The council agreed to it."

"I'm so glad. Thank you!" Putting her hand on his shoulder, she gave him a quick kiss. "Were they hard to persuade?"

He didn't say that her husband-to-be was the only council member who had voted against her plan. Why tell her something that would surely make her unhappy?

"They agreed to please their Brides. I'll show you how to work with the computer to order what you want. I'll have to approve everything."

She made a face. "I hope you're going to be reasonable."

"If not, I'm sure I can be cajoled."

"We're a lot of trouble to you, aren't we? Are you sorry you volunteered to be the Brides' liaison?" she asked.

His lips twitched as he recalled what he'd gone through to secure the appointment—the favors he'd called in, the politicking he'd done. "It's a lot of extra work but I don't mind it," he said, keeping his voice serious.

"Why do you smell so different today?" Janis asked as they continued down the corridor.

"I added an artificial layer, like human males wear. It smells like *zolicia* leaves," Delos said. *At least it covers Taddus' foul odor.*

She wrinkled her nose. "I prefer your natural scent."

"Thank you." No doubt she was unaware of it but she'd just paid him one of the highest compliments a female could give a male. "Your scent pleases me too," he said. "Especially when you're aroused."

A tinge of color suddenly flamed in her pale cheeks. Fascinated, he stopped and lifted her chin, the better to observe the phenomenon. "How did you do that?"

"What?"

"The lovely pink in your cheeks."

She put her palms to her face. "I must have blushed when you made that sexual remark."

He lowered his voice. "So if I said I like the way your nipples swell when I suck them, you might blush again?"

She turned away but not quickly enough. He saw the enchanting pink rise through her face. "Let's keep walking," she said. "I thought you were going to show me the ship."

* * * * *

Jan was amazed at the sheer size of *Ecstasy of Generations*. She'd gone on a singles cruise once—and had no luck—but this ship seemed to be much larger than that ocean-traveling Earth vessel.

Delos explained, "We recycle everything we can but some of it's inevitably lost to waste. There are only two stops between Teril and Gazeem, our new planet. So we have to carry or grow all of our food for the seven-year voyage."

"Gazeem?" It was the first time she'd heard the name of the planet they'd be colonizing.

"It's named after Primus Taddus' father. He was one of our greatest explorers."

As they took the shuttle to the shopping level of the ship, Jan asked, "Are your parents still alive?"

"My mother's on Teril." He looked out the window as the corridors flashed by. "My father was on the ship. He was one of those who died."

Jan knew him well enough now to read his expression. He was trying to keep his face blank but she sensed his sorrow. "I'm sorry," she said, her voice soft. "I lost my father a year ago. It's very difficult."

"The illness took my father, my brother, their wives, two of my sisters and my wife." He kept his face turned toward the window. "It's the same for all of us. Most were traveling in family groups. Almost everyone lost a father, a brother. Some of us had our young with us...all succumbed to the illness. And every female died as well."

His hands lay on his knees, the knuckles white. Tentatively she put her hand over his. His fingers gripped hers.

Concerned mainly with the kidnapping of her own kind, she hadn't thought much about the illness that had killed so many Terilians. Now, suddenly, it seemed personal. She tried to imagine going on a cruise with her whole family and losing them all at once. Would she have even wanted to go on living?

His voice was much lower as he added, "It was a hard time to be a doctor. They kept dying. No matter what I did, they died."

"Were you sick too?"

"No one escaped the illness. There were days I couldn't work. Couldn't leave my bed..." He looked down at their entwined hands, his brow creasing.

"On Earth, we have a name for what you're feeling. It's called survivor's guilt," Jan said. "I'm sure you did everything possible."

"Part of me knows that," he said quietly. "Part of me thinks I should have done more."

"I'm glad you lived."

He squeezed her hand. "I am too—now."

The shuttle halted. Delos kept hold of her hand as he led her to the corridor of shops.

Unlike Earth shops, with their brightly lit windows filled with merchandise, these stores consisted of a discreet length of plain gray corridor with small entrances every ten or twenty feet. Jan drew near and read the tiny sign, "Joyous Adornment. Restricted to primuses only."

"I can read this!" she exclaimed.

Delos took on a smug expression. "You don't think I'd have fitted you with an inferior brain chip, do you? You've gained both spoken and written language." He guided her to a tiny viewing window at eye level. "Look here to preview the merchandise."

She peered in at a lovely black tunic. The draped material was caught up on each shoulder by a decorative copper button. As Jan watched, the tunic turned slowly, showing the graceful folds of the front and back. When the rotation completed, the picture changed. Now she viewed herself wearing the garment.

As always, black was slimming. Jan said, "I wouldn't mind having a tunic like that."

Delos took a quick look. "Under our sumptuary laws, only primuses are permitted to wear gray or black." As they went to the next shop, he added, "Of course, you'll be a primus's wife. You'll be able to shop anywhere you want."

She looked up at him, caught by the pain and bitterness in his tone.

"I have to keep reminding myself," he told her, his voice grim. "I don't dare imagine that you could be mine permanently."

"Isn't there any way that we can be together?"

He looked into her eyes for a long moment. She felt sure he was going to tell her something. Then he said, "The primuses have first choice. In everything."

Why did she have the feeling he'd almost said something quite different?

Chapter Six

Delos gave her an appraising look. "You're probably not ready to do the jumps between floors. We'll use the elevator."

He took her to the recreation and exercise floor. Jan imagined the floor would be like a health club on Earth but it seemed that Terilians did not care for mindless, repetitive exercise. Many of their exercise routines engaged the mind as well as the body.

He showed her a large variety of virtual-reality games, usually played wearing full-body suits. Some of them were performed in low-gravity chambers, which looked especially entertaining.

Other games were played in large groups. Delos took her to an observation deck where they watched fifteen primuses, formed into three teams, play something that resembled "capture the flag".

"Do you ever play that?" Jan asked.

"The Medical Corps has four teams. I'm the captain of the doctors' team."

"Because you're the best player?"

"I'm not the best player." He grinned. "But I *am* the best strategist."

"What other games do you like?"

Delos led her to a small room that he said was a ball court. As Jan watched from an upper balcony, Delos stood in the center of the court, unsheathed his claws and said, "Ready!" Small, fluffy balls in various colors began to rain down from the ceiling. Spinning, turning, leaping, Delos caught them with his claws. A scoreboard on the far wall changed rapidly. "If I catch a blue one it counts against me, unless the lights are blinking," he called up to her, not pausing in his quick movements.

The game looked like fun but when he asked if she wanted to try it, Jan declined. She'd never been athletic and didn't want him to see how badly she'd do. Perhaps she would try it on her own, later.

He showed her sparring pits where males wearing gloves tipped with rubber claws fought each other. Jan couldn't figure out the rules as she watched two males in a free-for-all that combined wrestling, clawing and body blows, sometimes standing, sometimes rolling on the ground.

Jan didn't care for either boxing or wrestling on Earth but the sparring held her interest because it was so quick and graceful. The participants were like two dancers who had rehearsed with each other often and could anticipate the next movement.

Delos watched intently. Jan, startled, saw that his claws were extended. Somehow she'd never imagined the doctor as *dangerous* before.

"Good one!" he exclaimed as one male clawed the other's face. "That would've taken an eye in a real fight."

Jan shuddered. "Do you ever do that?"

"Not for real—but I spar with Hannus once a week."

She remembered the orderly who had helped her walk around the hospital room. "Hannus! He's twice your size."

Delos gave her a wicked grin. "Yes but I'm much faster."

As they left the sparring area, Jan saw a glass bulb on a silver stand, filled with tiny, multicolored spheres. Surely the Terilians hadn't developed human-style gumball machines. "What's this?"

"I'll buy a couple," Delos answered, waving his palm in front of the stand. A light came on briefly, then blue and gold spheres dropped from the machine. He handed her the blue one. "They're memory balls. Twist open and sniff."

Watching how the gold sphere separated under his grip, she followed his lead. The pungent odor of Gary's musky aftershave filled the room. The present seemed to fade away. Gary's beige and leather living room appeared in front of her eyes. Jan heard herself saying, "I'm just startled. We've only been on—what is it, six dates? I had no idea you felt like that about me."

Gary smiled. "I wouldn't waste my time going on all those dates with a woman who didn't interest me. Besides, we've worked together for two years. I know you're punctual, conscientious and an excellent programmer."

She laughed. "Are you looking for a wife—or a business partner?"

"Those traits form a sound basis for a good marriage," Gary answered earnestly. One of his faults, Jan had always thought, was that he lacked a sense of humor. "The other thing is, I don't want children. I figure at your age, you don't either."

She'd been about to protest, to say that she was only thirty-nine, when he took a small blue box out of his pocket. "Janis, will you marry me?"

This was what she'd waited for all her life, ever since she'd been a little girl playing "getting married" with one of her mother's lace curtains for a veil. "Yes," she breathed, leaning forward to see the small diamond. He gave her a quick peck on the mouth as the past faded…

"Did it work?" Delos asked her. His eyes were concerned as he looked into her face.

"Maybe too well."

He took her hand. His warm grip was comforting. "Not all memories are good ones."

Strange, she hadn't realized how very unromantic Gary's proposal had been until she relived it. The thought seemed to leave a bad taste in her mouth. "What memory did you experience?"

"A conversation with my wife." A crease appeared on his brow.

"Do you miss her?" Jan tried but couldn't keep the jealousy out of her voice.

"I did." He sighed. "It's been a long two years. We never dreamed we'd be trapped in this metal shell without our mates." He fell silent as they went down a long corridor.

"Where are we going now?" Jan asked after they'd walked for awhile without speaking.

"I want to show you the maze room," he said.

A hologram outside the door of the maze room showed the day's prize, a gold ankle bracelet. "We'll try this together," Delos said. "I'd like you to wear that." He rubbed his cheek against hers.

"You may as well forget it right now. I'm terrible at games."

"We'll see." The door closed behind them. "Wait for a moment until our eyes adjust."

She almost asked him tartly how they were expected to see in the dark. To her surprise, she began to make out dim shapes in the curtain of black that draped the room.

"The prize is somewhere in the center of the room but we can't go there directly," he explained. "If we choose the wrong path, we'll be dumped out of the maze."

He walked forward, leading her by the hand. Suddenly the ground slid beneath her feet. Jan almost fell but Delos steadied her. "Careful! We'll go slowly."

She breathed a sigh of relief when he put his arm around her waist, guiding her over the shifting ground.

"Stop!" he warned her. She looked down. The ground had ended, leaving them on the edge of a void.

"What now?" she asked.

"We wait."

She heard a soft sound as something approached them. A hovering platform drew near then stopped while it was five feet away.

"Now we're going to jump," he said.

"You're kidding, right?"

"You can do it. You're Terilian now."

She knew she still looked doubtful. He grinned. "I should know—I'm your doctor. I'll count to four and we'll leap."

He counted down and they jumped. To Jan's surprise, her legs were stronger than they'd ever been. The short leap was effortless. She landed on the platform with a foot to spare.

She clutched Delos' waist as the platform rose through the air. It took them to a dark area where they had to proceed single file.

"I'm not sure I like this," she said, stepping back to let him lead the way.

"Really? Terilians often seek out small, confined spaces." He walked forward with confidence. "They make us feel safe."

She followed him, staying close enough to touch him.

They came to a place where three corridors branched off in front of them. He checked out each entrance then said, "This way," heading to the right.

To her relief, the area soon widened and they were able to walk side-by-side again. She felt much more secure with his arm around her.

"Tunnel coming up," he warned.

Hesitantly she entered an even darker area. She raised her hand, feeling the top of the tunnel about a foot above her head.

Delos stopped walking. Had he sensed some new challenge?

Suddenly he gripped her around the waist. Pulling her close, he kissed her hungrily. Heat coiled in her loins. She closed her eyes and kissed him back, caressing his teeth with her tongue, moving her lips under his.

She basked in his warmth, inhaled his attractive cocoa scent but she couldn't see him at all. It was like being embraced by a phantom.

She felt him lift her tunic. Then his hand was on her mound, his fingers tangling in her curls. She let him touch her, enjoying how he stroked and rubbed her until she gasped with desperate arousal.

She heard steps in the distance, steps that drew nearer, then stopped.

"What if someone comes in?" she asked breathlessly.

"He'll envy me. I get to taste your beautiful nipples...like this..." His mouth was on her breast, his teeth nipping her gently through the fabric of her tunic. She threw her head back, panting.

Eyes were watching them from the dark. Lustful eyes. She opened her mouth to ask Delos to stop but all that emerged was a long moan of pleasure.

He murmured into her breasts, telling her how beautiful she was, how much he longed to mount her, how the aroma of her sex excited him. She ached for him to touch her harder, deeper.

Eyes shone out of the dark at the entrance to the tunnel. Yellow eyes. Did she recognize the scent? She couldn't think about it. All she wanted was more pleasure.

He jerked her tunic open at the shoulder. His mouth closed over her right breast. He drew the nipple into his mouth, flicking it again and again with his tongue.

"More, Delos!" She squirmed against his hand.

Delos entered her with one finger. She put her hands on his shoulders, bracing herself and parted her thighs.

"I love touching you. I love feeling your cream on my hand," he whispered.

"Yes! You make me so wet."

He thrust deeper. She gasped and moved against him.

She couldn't believe she was letting him do this to her in public. Anyone might be nearby. But his touch was so stimulating, so pleasurable…

He moved his hand faster. She bucked against him, frantic. What kind of woman had she turned into, to do this here?

A woman desperate for sex. Desperate for his hands, his mouth.

When she came, it was quick and sharp. She wanted so badly to make noise but the thought of that was embarrassing, so she buried her cries in Delos' shoulder. He held her tightly, his cheek against her hair.

"You're mine, Janis," Delos said. "Do you understand? Mine."

Was he speaking to her, or to the unseen watcher?

A faint growl emerged from the darkness. Had Delos heard? If so, he ignored it.

Quickly, Jan pulled down her tunic. "Let's go. I wouldn't want anyone else to know what we did in there." It had been too dark for anyone else to really see anything, she told herself.

She thought she heard Delos chuckle as they made their way out of the tunnel and down the next corridor. To her relief, this one was well-lit. "What's so funny?" she asked.

"You're still thinking like a human. We're not in the tunnel any longer but—scents linger." He smiled. "You're blushing again."

She didn't answer, just kept hurrying along the corridor. When it branched four ways, Delos let her choose. Unfortunately, her choice led to an exit door.

"We lost," Delos said, his tone disappointed. "I wanted you to win the prize."

She stopped to kiss him. "I did win a prize—in the tunnel."

Solange Ayre

* * * * *

The day after Delos showed her around the ship, Janis announced to the Brides that there would be a wedding ceremony. The Brides divided into committees. Computer interfaces were set up in the Great Hall and each committee uplinked with the master computer to plan clothing, music, the feast and the vows.

Several days passed while the committees worked. The food committee came up with a menu and then interacted with the computer to find Terilian equivalents. The vows committee squabbled endlessly about the wording. The music committee faced problems too, as everyone had different ideas as to what was suitable and no one seemed to know all the words to the Chicken Dance.

Arguments about liquor raged until they discovered the Terilians didn't drink. Instead they filled little bags with a fragrant herb and inhaled. Jan requested that *niphela* be brought to the Great Hall. Many women doubted that it would affect them but it turned out they'd become sufficiently Terilian to get a pleasant buzz from the herb. Half a day was wasted in experimenting with the substance.

Everything they requested had to be overseen by Delos but that wasn't a problem. Approvals came through so quickly that Jan suspected he hadn't even listened to them — wherever he was keeping himself. He hadn't been near her in several days. She wondered what he was doing and why he hadn't tried to see her.

One afternoon, Jan was enjoying a hot-chocolate-like beverage and small, meat-filled rolls with the rest of the Brides when a rolling messenger entered the Great Hall. The tiny machine stopped at the doorway. "Janis Stone, you are summoned," it announced.

She followed it out into the corridor, hoping the summons had come from Delos. "Where are we going?" she asked.

"To Primus Taddus' cabin."

Chapter Seven

Jan's apprehension grew as she paced after the messenger. Delos had said everyone had sworn not to have intercourse until the Spring Running. Did that include the primuses? Or would Taddus try to force himself on her?

Rape is impossible in our culture. Delos had said that too. But her growing fear made his earlier statement difficult to believe.

Taddus was standing impatiently in the doorway of his cabin as she approached. He smiled when he saw her. His yellow eyes seemed to search every inch of her body, lingering on her breasts and her pelvis.

"Janis, please come in. I thought we should have a talk before the Spring Running."

She hesitated. "On Earth, women don't enter the homes of men they don't know."

"The messenger shall stay, if you like." He bent and addressed the machine. "Bear witness that I will do nothing to the human woman without her consent."

"Witness function activated." The machine rolled into a corner and extended a blinking glass lens.

Jan entered his cabin. It was three times the size of hers, with heavy, wooden furniture that was permanently affixed to the deck. One entire wall showed changing pictures, like the corridors. Jan assumed they were scenes from Teril.

"Please—be seated," Taddus said, bringing out a stool for her.

Jan sat, arranging her tunic over her knees. She was very conscious of the sheer material she wore.

He stared at her nipples. "Your soft breasts entice me, Janice. Perhaps you'll let me lick and suck them."

She tossed her hair. "I came here to talk. That's all."

He turned and paced toward the bed. "You've been spending much of your time with Secondus Delos."

"Delos and I have become good friends," Jan answered.

"Not surprising. Everyone likes Del. He's considered quite brilliant in his field, you know."

"I didn't know. He doesn't speak of himself much."

"The cream of Teril was chosen for this colonization venture. The best Teril had to offer." Coming closer, he put his hand on her shoulder. She inhaled, trying to decide what she thought of his scent. "So I understand your liking for the young doctor. But primuses have first choice and I have chosen you as my Bride."

Perhaps this was her chance. "You may have chosen me but I haven't chosen you."

He laughed indulgently. "But you will, my dear. When I come for you at the Spring Running, you'll be happy to mate with me. And I will be proud to be married to the most beautiful Earth woman on the ship. Now, let us talk and get to know each other's essences. Once you know me better, I'm sure you will be pleased to be my wife."

She tilted her head, considering his words. "Go ahead. *Talk* all you want." She already knew that nothing could make her choose him rather than Delos.

He smiled, entirely missing her sarcasm. "Not only beautiful but a female of sense." He brought another stool close to hers.

He told her of his family's glorious heritage, the exploits of his explorer father, Gazeem, the beauty and wit of his mother, Alora, the fame and intelligence of his siblings. He spoke at length of his years at school, his training in governance, the prizes he'd won for his carefully reasoned papers. He talked about the wife he'd brought on board with him and how happy she'd been, married to a primus and a council member.

Jan felt like she was on a bad date with a man who wouldn't let her get a word in edgewise.

At last he rose, saying he had something to show her. She took the opportunity to say, "Taddus? Wouldn't you like to hear about my life on Earth?"

Turning back quickly, he said, "Janis, you're Terilian now. I believe the sooner you forget your old, primitive life, the better." He opened a metal chest and lifted out a copper necklace. "I'd like you to wear this. Consider it the first of many gifts you will receive, as the wife of Primus Taddus."

"Perhaps you should wait until we're married." Panic shot through her as he lowered the heavy necklace over her hair.

"No, I wish to see you wearing this lavish gift." Taking her hands, he helped her to her feet. "It enhances your beauty, my dear." Keeping hold of her hand with his left, he stroked her cheek with his right. "As my wife, you'll enjoy the best quarters, the best food. You'll be richly dressed at all times. You'll never have to work."

"I might want to work," Jan suggested.

"But you won't, my dear. Your days will be spent in leisure. All males will envy me—even the other primuses."

His hand moved down her neck, stroking, caressing. She shivered. Like Delos, he was touching her gently, trying to give her pleasure. But she felt no response.

"Let me touch your breast," he murmured.

She hesitated. But after all, why not? If she had to marry him, she might as well see what he was like. "You may touch me," she said.

He rubbed his cheek against hers affectionately. Why did it mean so much more when Delos did it? His fingers went to her breasts, circling the nipples, attempting to stimulate her through the sheer fabric.

Taddus' hands were skillful but he might as well have been a doctor giving her a breast examination. She wasn't interested.

To stop him, she put her hands to his face. He turned his head, licking her palm. If Delos had done the same thing, she would have trembled with delight. When Taddus did it, she wanted to wipe her palm.

"Taddus, I don't want to marry you."

His smile was patronizing. "All females are nervous prior to the Spring Running, Janis. Once we've mated, you'll be content—you'll see."

"There are almost a thousand other Brides on the ship. Choose another. Choose someone who will be proud to be your wife." She took a deep breath. "Let me have the husband I want."

"You only think you want Del. You'll forget all about him after the Spring Running. Glorious beauty like yours must not be wasted on a mere secondus." He patted her cheek. "A year from now, we'll look back on this conversation and laugh."

"You're not listening to me. Do you really want an unwilling wife?"

"But you won't be unwilling, sweet Janis. You'll enjoy our many matings at the Spring Running."

She bit back bitter words. There was simply nothing she could say that he'd hear. "I'm leaving."

He glanced at the silently witnessing machine, then stood back to allow her access to the door. "Of course, my dear." He followed her to the door. His hand was on his groin, rubbing the head of his cock through his tunic. "Leave now if you will. There will be no leaving on the day I take you again and again. I'll make you beg and plead for every thrust of my penis."

Jan's voice went deep and low. She had never spoken with more truthfulness in her life. "Primus, I will *die* before I beg you for anything."

One Thousand Brides

* * * * *

Delos was working at the computer console in his quarters when the door announced that Janis Stone wished to enter. Jumping to his feet, he commanded the door to open.

She walked in. He was familiar with her expressions now and knew that she was angry.

Her tunic was pink today, a color that emphasized her pale skin and dark hair. Then he noticed the heavy copper necklace she wore and frowned.

"You've been with Taddus." He smelled the primus's odor on her neck.

She tossed her head and her glorious black hair rippled in waves. "He called me to his cabin. Why shouldn't he? If I'm his destined Bride, I'll soon be spending *all* my days with him."

Rage shot through him at the thought of the primus touching her. He stepped closer to her and reached around her neck. Grasping the clasp of the necklace, he broke it with one sharp tug and threw the necklace to the floor.

She stared at him, eyes wide. In another moment they were in each other's arms.

His mouth took hers savagely. He wanted to devour her lips and tongue. He wanted to lick her everywhere — her neck, her nipples and most of all her aroused sex.

When they finally broke apart, gasping, she gazed up at him fiercely. "Where have you been?" she demanded. "I haven't seen you for days!"

She missed me. She longed for me. Her words were so meaningful to him that he had to kiss her again.

"I've been working triple shifts," he said. "Every male on the ship needs extra anti-erection drugs. The presence of so many unmated females is driving us all mad."

She put her hand on his erect penis. "Physician, heal yourself."

He laughed at the apt phrase. "I took drugs two hours ago. They don't help when you're so close." He called the bed out and down to the floor. "Even if we can't mate, let me hold you." He stretched out on the bed, waiting.

She hesitated, then lay beside him. "Really, what's the use? If we can't marry, aren't we just torturing ourselves?"

"Sweet torture," he groaned, licking the side of her face. Her skin was fresh and soft. He couldn't think about the future, only the joy of holding her now. "Let's enjoy each other while we can."

"It's foolish."

"It's not foolish." He licked her nipple through the sheer material. "It's love."

She gazed at him, a beautiful, soft look coming into her eyes. "Really, Delos? You *love* me?"

"From the day I first saw you." He gave her another kiss. Her lips parted and her tongue stroked his. Kissing had felt so strange at first but the more he did it, the more he liked it. What else would she teach him?

"Loving the way I look isn't loving *me*," she said, her voice low. "You don't know very much about me. How can you talk about love?"

"I know plenty about you."

"You know I'm under forty, childless, fertile and not pair-bonded," she said, quoting from Taddus' criteria for the kidnapped females.

He smiled. "And you enjoy sarcasm. I'll tell you what else I know... You lived in several multi-unit dwellings until three years ago, when you bought your own living quarters. You had two of the Earth animals called 'cats' as pets. Last year you took an evening class in something called 'Ceramics'. You spent more than one percent of your compensation last year on reading material and music."

She stared at him for a moment, looking puzzled. Then her brow smoothed. "Oh—that's right, you said your people uploaded data on all the Brides. You must have read my computer records."

Read them? He'd practically memorized every tiny detail the data yielded. Every aspect of her fascinated him.

He wished he'd known her for years. He could have loved her when they were gawky adolescents together, before she grew into the breathtaking beauty who had attracted Primus Taddus' notice.

"If we were married, I'd have you tell me something different about you every day. We'd record it on the computer so our young could hear about your life."

"So you'd actually want to hear about my 'old, primitive' life on Earth?"

"I want to hear everything. Because I love you."

She snuggled against him, rubbing her face against his neck. "Let me do something to please you. Please let me try," she begged. "Maybe it won't work. But I'd love to give you an orgasm."

He raised his eyebrows, wondering what she was thinking. "Go ahead."

"Lie on your back."

He stretched out.

"Open your legs," she told him. When he did, she knelt between them. As always when he was with her for any length of time, his organ was erect.

Holding his penis by the base, she lowered her head and took it in her mouth. She closed her lips around the head. He raised up on his shoulders, watching as she pumped her hand up and down. Her lips traveled over his shaft, sucking hard.

The sensation was incredible. He knew he wouldn't be able to experience an orgasm this way. But her hand and mouth on his penis, both at the same time, was one of the most pleasurable things he'd ever experienced. He shook and gasped as her hand moved faster and her hot mouth took him deeper.

Her lips, slick and wet, stroked his long shaft. He felt himself growing, swelling even larger. She was doing her best and the pleasure was intense — almost unbearable.

"If only I could mount you now," he gasped. "Janis — stop. I can't take any more."

She raised her head, sorrow in her eyes. "I wish I could give you an orgasm."

He said sadly, "It's not your fault, beautiful one. Terilian males just aren't made that way." As she moved up close to him, he stroked her cheek. "I've never had such pleasure from a female's mouth before."

"I can hardly wait until the Spring Running. I want to have sex with you. I want you to have an orgasm while you're inside me." She kissed him, then murmured against his mouth, "I want to make you happy."

He caressed her nipples through her tunic, rolling them between his fingers until her breathing changed to short gasps. "Then tell me you love me," he demanded.

"I...I don't know what to say." Her eyes avoided his.

"Tell me."

"It's too soon. Don't press me."

He stroked her face again. "Turn on your stomach and raise up on your knees and elbows. I want to give you pleasure."

She sat up, shaking her long hair back, gazing at him doubtfully.

"Trust me."

She did as he asked. Hungrily he stared at her. Inside her tunic, her breasts hung freely. In this position, they looked ripe and luscious, like *polchoi* ready to drop from the tree.

He raised the hem of her tunic, exposing the darkening, swelling lips of her vagina.

His organ quivered. She was in the prime position to be mounted.

Coming up behind her on his knees, he said, "Remember this position. When we meet at the Spring Running, I'll take you this way first." He put his hands on her butt cheeks, rubbing them, squeezing them until she moaned.

Her lovely anus seemed to beg to be touched. He circled it with his thumb, teasing the tender flesh at its perimeter.

"Delos!"

"Don't you like that?"

"I'm not sure. No one's ever touched me there before."

"I'll stop anytime you say."

She was silent, so he continued rubbing his thumb over the puckered hole. Then he slid his fingers up her labia.

"You're wet for me," he said. "You're always soft when I touch you. And so wet."

Her voice shook. "I love it when you touch me."

He fondled her anus again, his thumb pushing against it. She whimpered as half an inch of his thumb penetrated her. "Is that all right?"

"It hurts a little." Her voice was breathy. "But I-I kind of like it anyway."

Keeping his thumb in the tight hole, he softly stroked her labia over and over. When she began moving against his hand, he decided to try a different type of stimulation.

Reluctantly he took his hands off her body to reposition himself, smiling when she gave a soft, "Oh!" of disappointment.

"Hush, you'll like this," he murmured.

He knelt lower, bringing his face to her sex. The scent of her arousal drove him mad. How would he ever wait until the Spring Running?

He lapped at her hot, swollen lips with his tongue, then reached around and brushed her clitoris with his hand. The tiny bud was already hard and swollen. She pushed against him, wordlessly demanding more. He massaged her peak with two fingers, smiling when she jerked her hips and moaned.

Holding her lips apart with his fingers, he plunged his tongue into her tight, hot channel. He thrust again and again, pushing deep inside her. Her body shook and trembled. Lapping her freely flowing juices, he gloried in the knowledge that he could evoke this response from her. Was anything better than giving a dear one pleasure?

She cried out, convulsing against his mouth, rocking her hips hard. Her excited cries filled the room as her orgasm pulsed, an earthquake followed by tremors and aftershocks.

When it was finally over, she turned and stretched out on the bed. He followed her down, satisfied with the joy he'd given her. She nestled against him and stroked his chest.

He was half-dozing, enjoying her stimulating touch, when she whispered, "Delos? I love you."

His arm tightened around her. *She loves me.* Elation brimmed within his chest.

He knew then what he had to do.

* * * * *

Inevitably, there were setbacks with the wedding plans. The Brides were dismayed to find there were no flowers on the ship, nor was there wax for candles. The clothing committee was bitterly divided over whether white should be worn, some saying that white was for virgins only, others sneering and saying that was an old-fashioned idea.

Most women wanted rings for both Brides and grooms but Jan had learned that only primus males were allowed to wear jewelry.

One woman proposed that the primuses have a separate wedding from the seconduses. "Their whole society is structured like that. Why not?" she asked.

"We should maintain solidarity as human women!" another woman argued. "I say one wedding!"

A vote was taken, with the decision narrowly falling on the side of one wedding.

Jan asked that all the women's belongings be brought to the Great Hall. An hour later, six burly crew members carried in large metal pallets. The computer chose eighteen women at random and they went through the pallets, laughing and chattering as though it were a seventy-five percent off sale at Macy's.

When Jan's wedding dress was held up, everyone in the Great Hall fell silent. Jan gazed at the lovely gown, wondering if Gary regretted her disappearance. Had he found another woman to marry? Perhaps his secretary—that bitch had always been after him.

"You'll have a real wedding gown," Beth said enviously. "The only one." Although the young redhead hadn't cried in days, Jan knew the young woman still mourned the loss of her wedding on Earth. "You're so lucky... I hear you're going to marry Primus Taddus. He's the head honcho, so you'll be like the queen, right?"

"*If* I marry him," Jan murmured. She walked past the piles of clothing. An amazing array of items had come out of the women's purses—novels, candy bars, makeup, brushes and combs. Someone had brought perfume samples in small tearable packets. Jan took several, tucking them into her shoes.

She was the only woman here who was assured of marrying a primus. As she watched the others laughing and chattering, she thought, *I'm the only one here dreading the ceremony.*

*****

Jan dreamed that Delos was with her in bed. His mouth was hot and urgent on her breasts. His cock nudged her entrance as he lay between her legs. Her pussy swelled, begging for his touch. She stroked his beautiful soft hair, so happy he was with her again...

"All Brides report to the fourteenth floor. Follow the blinking corridor lights to the central elevators. All Brides..."

Desolated, Jan tore herself away from the dream. The dulcet voice of the computer continued as she rose and threw a flame-red tunic over her head.

The Brides babbled questions as they met up in the corridors. Many asked Jan if she knew what was happening. She answered that she knew no more than anyone else.

But in her heart, she knew this had to be the Spring Running.

"You wouldn't believe the dream I was having just now," one woman giggled.

"Me too!"

Jan saw Beth nearby, a dreamy expression on her face. The young woman reached up and fondled her own breasts as she hurried to the elevator.

Jan looked away. She would have liked to touch herself too. Her nipples ached and her pussy was drenched with need.

Stop thinking about sex.

She had used some of her time with the computer to learn everything she could about the ship. The fourteenth floor was the agricultural level. Here the crops were grown that fed everyone aboard. There was also a parklike area with grasslands and trees.

The women gasped in wonder as they emerged from the central elevators. After the narrow metal corridors of the ship's residential area, the acres of red and green plants were startling. Jan breathed in the intoxicating scents of growing things, tilled soil and rainwater.

The council was present, kneeling on their customary stools. The secondus males were already gathered together, their eyes hungrily devouring the Brides. Jan looked for Delos but couldn't find him in the crowd.

Council member Goldus rose to address them.

"Beautiful Brides, welcome to one of the most important events of the Terilian people. You may have noticed yourself experiencing intense erotic longings recently. You're merely responding to our male pheromones and to your own desires to mate during today's Spring Running.

"When the whistle sounds, run deep into the park and conceal yourselves. At the end of twenty minutes, the secondus-ranked males will search for you. Don't make it too easy for them, Brides! Part of the joy of the Spring Running is the challenge of finding you before mating.

"After another hour, the fifty primus-ranked males will be allowed into the park. Be aware that primuses have first choice among females, so even if you've already mated with a secondus, you may still be fortunate enough to gain a primus husband."

Janis' gaze strayed to Primus Taddus. His eyes were fixed on her.

Behind him she recognized Hannus, the aide who had helped her in the hospital. As they locked glances, he licked his lips.

The secondus males would seek them first. But what if another secondus male reached her before Delos?

Her body was ripe for pleasure. She wanted sex far more than she'd ever wanted food during her long, miserable diet.

But she didn't want just any male. She wanted Delos.

Goldus concluded, "May the Great Fur-Mother bless us all today. Brides, good Running."

The whistle sounded. The Brides, looking hesitantly at each other, moved into the park.

"Run, ladies!" Jan shouted. Somehow she knew what to do almost by instinct. This would be a joyous game, a hide-and-seek spectacular with mating as the glorious prize.

Throwing her head back, she ran. Warm artificial light beat down from the violet-painted ceiling. She moved effortlessly, head high. Surely her legs had never been so strong before. She laughed in sheer delight and heard the same from other women.

They ran tirelessly, spreading out as they moved farther into the park. Jan searched for a place to hide. There were many copses of tall grasses but she wanted to find someplace where she could watch for Delos' arrival.

At last she spotted a tree with a low-hanging branch. Certain she'd be able to reach it, she took a running leap. Breathlessly she caught the trunk with her claws as she steadied herself on the branch.

She'd done it and was now six feet high in the tree.

You're becoming more Terilian every day. The thought didn't bother her the way it had at the beginning. She'd grown accustomed to her enhanced sense of smell, her increased strength, even her claws.

And, just like a Terilian female, she was ready to mate. Without conscious thought, she raised her tunic and massaged her mound. Her hand slipped against her slick juices. Had she ever been so wet before? She'd certainly never wanted to come so badly before.

Balanced on the tree branch, she couldn't touch herself the way she needed. Couldn't open her legs far enough.

God, she wanted Delos' cock inside her, moving in and out, fucking her. Deep and hard. So hard...

The scents changed. She peered out eagerly, noting a number of shapes moving through the grasslands.

The males are entering the park.

She took a deep scenting of the air, hoping to find Delos. The threads of other scents unraveled in her mind and she identified Hannus.

What would she do if he reached her first?

In the distance she heard a breathless laugh and a deeper groan. Then the high, excited trills of a woman enjoying the hard thrusts of a male's lusty cock.

One of her fellow humans had already found a mate. Jan envied her.

Where is Delos?

"Yes! Harder!" A woman's voice came faintly to her ears.

She stroked her nether lips with one finger. She was gushing with arousal, shaking with anticipation. She closed her eyes and pictured Delos' big cock. Would the cylindrical head feel strange inside her pussy? Or would it give her even greater pleasure than a human male's penis?

Her nipples tightened with desire. Heat ignited through her pussy.

The males were close enough to see now. They were naked except for red cords around their loins which kept their erections close to their bodies, supporting their cocks as they ran.

Hannus drew near. "Janis?" he called in his gruff voice. "I scent you. Let me mount your sweet sex."

Her eyes widened as her pussy pulsed. His scent was irresistible. She gazed down at his large erection. How wonderful it would feel as he pumped in and out of her.

"Janis, I want to spread you open and thrust into you over and over. I promise you'll enjoy it."

She knew she would. She wanted to jump down from the tree, throw herself into the soft grass and open her legs wantonly.

She had to mate.

Where was Delos?

Chapter Eight

Wait for Delos. She stayed quiet.

Hannus peered up into the tree. "Janis!" He fumbled with his cord, staring up at her. She looked down into his yellow eyes, a bird caught in a snake's gaze.

A rustle came from behind her, breaking the spell. Jan's nostrils were suddenly full of a distinct cocoa scent.

"Find another female." Delos' voice was quiet but firm. "Janis is mine."

Hannus turned but didn't back away. "Go away, Del. I was here first."

Delos leaped at him. Faster than Janis' eyes could follow, Delos raised his arm. A moment later, blood ran from a long scratch on Hannus' chest.

"First cut," Delos said. Hannus growled and slunk away.

Don't make it too easy for them. Remembering Goldus' advice, Janis jumped down from the tree. A bubble of happiness swelled inside her as she ran.

She giggled as she brushed by long leaves of grass. Delos followed swiftly. She glanced back once. The eager look on his beloved face made her heart skip a beat. What would he do when he caught her?

No one had ever wanted her like this before.

Her heart pounded as he grasped her around the waist. She stumbled—or had he tripped her?—and they rolled to the ground.

She wanted him—God, how she wanted him—but a Terilian female always fought. She elbowed him and rolled away, breathless, trying to get to her feet. Swiftly, he caught her from behind. His palms captured her breasts.

His hands were rough, squeezing, groping. Her nipples were instantly erect. She opened her mouth, tempted to shamelessly beg him to fuck her.

She made one last effort, jerking away and trying to flee.

He caught her leg and pulled her down underneath him. Wriggling, she struggled to free herself. He subdued her easily, his arms like steel bands. She ended up face down, panting, while he straddled her butt, pinning her down with strong thighs.

I'm helpless. He can do whatever he wants to me. The thought was so stimulating that her pussy throbbed.

Moving her hair, he licked her neck. She moaned, all thought of resistance disappearing.

She was wild with arousal, pulsing with eagerness. She'd die if he didn't put his cock inside her.

She felt him shift as he unwound his cord, freeing his organ. His excited growl rumbled through the air. He raised up, giving her room to move. "Spread your legs."

She hurried to take the mating position, raising her hips, opening her legs. He came up behind her on his knees, hands gripping her hips, pushing the big, cylindrical head of his cock against her pussy lips. She was ready and wet and eager.

"Janis," he groaned and slid his cock inside her with one powerful thrust. Her vagina thrilled at the invasion. She moaned as her slick channel pulsed around his size and heat.

He plunged deep. He was so big, filling her in a way she'd never known. Her pussy gushed with liquid, welcoming him.

He pulled all the way out and that back-stroke was even better than his first hard thrust. Every nerve pleaded for more. He plunged into her again, frantically and she had to cry out. Leaning forward, he bit her shoulder. Pain mingled with pleasure as her pussy contracted.

He thrust fast and hard, pounding her with his thick organ as her juices spurted against him, easing the tight passage.

Pleasure built and built each time he moved. She had one brief thought that others might be nearby. Then she lost all worry about that. Every one of his fierce thrusts demanded that she cry out in response. She gasped and moaned mindlessly, waiting for the orgasm she knew he would give her.

His cock was buried deeply inside her. He reached underneath her and took her nipples with his fingers, rolling and rubbing them.

The extra stimulation was everything she needed. Racking waves of pure delight flooded her pelvis and she clenched against his steel-hard cock over and over. Her orgasm radiated through every inch of her sensitized pussy.

"*Mine!*" he growled, triumph filling his voice. His hips jerked and he shouted aloud. All her senses told her that he'd come.

* * * * *

Delos watched Janis slump forward, panting with the force of her orgasm.

He sank into a kneeling position. Never before had sex satisfied him so completely.

He gazed down at his half-erect cock, coated with her juices. Janis had been even more incredible than he'd hoped. Their mating had been soul-satisfying. When he achieved orgasm, he felt as though she'd drained every drop from him.

She was human, he was Terilian. Yet when he'd filled her with his penis, he'd felt that he was part of her. Or as though they were both parts of one being, finally whole.

Her dark hair was disheveled. Her tunic was pushed up past her waist, leaving her lovely naked buttocks exposed to his gaze.

His organ stiffened. Urgency filled him.

"Janis—again." He waited with a touch of apprehension. Had he shocked her?

"Yes!" She rose up and parted her thighs. The scent of her aroused sex made him mindless with lust. His organ was hard and throbbing, more than ready to plunge inside her again. It took every bit of control he had but he delayed, rubbing the head against her labia.

She moaned, trying to thrust her sex against his organ. "Delos! I want you!"

"What do you want?" He teased her, letting his organ slip an inch into her wet channel, then withdrawing. She raised her hips, desperately trying to take his penis inside her.

"Mount me again. Now, Delos! I can't wait!"

He thrust into her, moving with fast, shallow strokes this time. The tight walls of her vagina clung around his organ, caressing and milking him until he thought he couldn't bear the searing pleasure.

She moved with his quick rhythm. "Harder!" she gasped.

Instead he stopped moving, his eyes half-closing, drinking in the sensation of her tight channel clutched around his organ.

"Don't stop!" she pleaded.

"Move for me," he ordered her.

Hesitantly, she rocked back against him, then forward. "That's right, that's good," he gasped, encouraging her. She moved again, harder this time. He held still, letting her plunge against his stiff penis, taking it as hard as she wanted. Taking it deep.

He groaned as she thrust faster and faster, rutting against him wildly, her channel like a hot, wet pleasure device made for his organ alone.

His palms massaged her buttocks, heightening their excitement. She screamed and clamped down around him.

White-hot cum shot from the base of his penis and up his shaft like liquid fire. He'd never felt such pure, whole sensation before.

Finally his organ receded. She pulled forward, breathing hard and lay on her side. He stretched out beside her, stroking her flushed cheek, then gave her one of those wet human kisses she liked so much.

I like them too, he thought as her tongue glided languidly against his.

He had to take her again. Maybe from the front this time, so he could watch her beautiful breasts quiver as he thrust into her deliciously hot, clinging sex.

He cupped her right breast in his hand, enjoying the softness against his palm.

"I thought of a way to defeat Taddus," she said.

His eyes flew open.

She pulled away from his arms and grabbed one of her shoes, lifting something out of it. "Look!" She held it under his nose. Even though the package was sealed, he smelled the sweet aroma. "If we rub this on our skin, it'll change our scents. Taddus won't be able to find us."

What an incredible female she was. Not only beautiful…not only his perfect mate…but wonderfully clever.

A pity her plan wouldn't work.

"Taddus won't track you by scent, the way I did," he explained. "The primuses follow computer links to their chosen females."

"That seems like cheating."

"It's our way."

Trouble darkened her gaze. "Then there's no escape from him?"

He didn't answer, just pulled her back into his arms and kissed her until they were both gasping with arousal.

"I don't know what's the matter with me," she murmured. "I want you again. *Now*."

"Then make me hard." He rose to his feet. "Suck me."

Eagerly she knelt in front of him, grasping the base of his organ. Her beautiful rosy lips closed around the head and she stroked him with her tongue.

She gently cupped his testicles, rolling his sac as her mouth caressed him. She sucked him, devouring him as his pleasure built. His organ stiffened. He cried out hoarsely and she made a delighted noise in her throat.

"Lie on your back," he said. She lay in the grass, her thighs parted. The smile she gave him filled his heart with joy. Stroking his hard penis, he gazed down at her.

She'd always been beautiful but now, with her skin flushed with pleasure and her nipples and vagina still swollen from their mating, she was breathtaking. He knelt between her thighs. His inflamed organ demanded that he thrust into her again but he paused to kiss her mouth and her breasts. She whispered his name, stimulating him further.

He raised her legs onto his shoulders and thrust deep. His hard, hot penis slid easily into her wet channel. He rocked back and forth inside her, watching her white breasts quiver as he thrust and withdrew, thrust and withdrew.

"I never knew it could be like this," she whispered.

"I didn't either." His palms traveled up and down her soft thighs. "I want to give you more pleasure, beautiful one."

"I'm so close!" she gasped.

He moved his hand to where they were joined and fondled her swollen clitoris with his thumb. Her eyes flew open. She cried out, her back arching, her hips bucking. He felt her tight spasms clenching against his organ. Pleasure wrenched a shout from his throat as she screamed.

Janis lay half-dozing against Delos' chest, worn out from the three orgasms that had filled her with unbelievable pleasure. Their mating had been so beautiful...but soon it would be over. She'd be another male's wife. Delos would never hold her again, or kiss her, or make love to her.

"He's near," Delos said quietly.

She jumped to her feet, extending her claws.

"Put your claws away," he told her. His eyes were shadowed.

"Are you leaving now?" Desolation flooded her.

He rose easily to his feet and rubbed his face against hers. "Whatever happens, remember I love you."

Suddenly alarmed, she asked, "What are you going to do?"

There was no time to answer as Taddus loped up before them and released his cord. His dark organ was swollen, the head purple with arousal.

In a few minutes, the primus would use that organ on her. She shuddered with dread.

The primus's tongue passed over his lips. He looked at her, slowly stroking the head of his penis. "My wife." Taddus' tone was formal. "Janis Stone, I am here to claim you."

Delos' tone was equally formal as he took one step forward. "Primus Taddus, I refuse to yield her to you."

Jan gasped. So he wasn't going to merely hand her over to the higher-ranked male. He loved her enough to face down the big primus.

A thrill ran through her.

Taddus stared at him. "Are you *challenging* me, Delos? You're insane! Seek another mate!"

"You know our law. It's my right as a secondus to fight for this one."

Taddus lowered his head and growled. Jan's hand flew to her mouth. Slender Delos had to weigh fifty pounds less than Taddus. How could he possibly defeat the primus?

Delos growled back, a terrifying rumble. "State the rules, Primus."

"Claws permitted, no biting, no foreign objects," Taddus said. "We fight until one of us yields."

"Agreed." The two males glared at each other. Delos planted his feet and raised his hands, palm outward. Taddus did the same. They locked fingers and counted together, "Four…three…two…one!"

They unsheathed their claws. Agony washed over both males' faces as their claws dug into each other's hands.

Jan's heart galloped with fright as they tumbled to the ground. Delos, on top, got his right hand free. He swiped at Taddus' face. The primus threw himself clear and rolled, switching their positions.

"No female is worth this!" Taddus hissed. "Yield, Delos!"

Delos clawed Taddus' back. "First cut!"

"Fool!" Rage bellowed from Taddus' throat. "I have twice your strength!" The two males twisted and struggled, their growls growing more fierce. They rolled over and over, kicking and clawing. Jan watched, afraid to make a sound, fearing to distract Delos.

Taddus' back was bleeding. Delos didn't make a sound as Taddus scraped three claws down his chest.

Taddus, on top now, achieved a hold on both of Delos' wrists and forced Delos' hands to the ground.

Jan's heart sank. Taddus sneered, "Yield and I won't hurt you, little secondus."

Delos remained silent. Sweat beaded on his brow and shoulders. Blood dripped slowly from the wounds on his chest.

Taddus brought his face closer and threatened, "I'll notch your ear."

Delos' ears twitched. "Rules!" he gasped. "No biting!"

Taddus laughed. His lips pulled back, revealing his sharp fangs. "Yield!" he commanded.

"Not—to a cheater!" Delos panted.

The big primus lowered his head.

Would Taddus really mutilate Delos? Unbidden, a low growl emerged from Jan's throat. She leaped forward, grabbing Taddus around the neck. Her claws sank into his flesh. Blood welled and he shouted in pain.

For a moment, the two males stared at her with identical, shocked expressions.

Then Taddus' hands shot up as he tried to free himself from her claws. Delos, suddenly loosened from Taddus' grasp, slashed the other male across the face.

"My eye!" Taddus shrieked, his hand covering it.

"Yield!" Delos panted. "Go to Sick Bay—save your eye!" He jumped to his feet, standing over the kneeling primus.

Taddus glared at Jan. "You broke our law! Females don't interfere with challenges!"

"Guess what?" She lowered her face to his. "Human females do."

Their gazes locked. Jan raised her hands again. Her claws were slick with his blood.

"I yield." Taddus' voice was sullen. "Keep your savage female, Delos."

Delos pulled Jan close and possessively rubbed his face against hers. "I intend to."

*****

The Brides straggled back to the Great Hall with their new husbands, each couple tied together at the wrist with the red cords, male's right hand to Bride's left. The Brides reluctantly left their mates just long enough to dress in their wedding garb. An anxious Jan talked to many of the women, relieved when it became clear that they were happy with their new husbands.

"I've never had an orgasm with a lover before," one woman confided in her. "Terilian males really know how to please their mates."

"Don't I know it," Jan answered with a smile.

Beth strolled into the Hall by Taddus' side. The big male had bandages on his eye and neck.

"I waited forever. I thought no one would choose me," Beth whispered to Jan. "I was so pleased when Taddus came!" She linked her arm through his. "I know we're going to be happy together." She gazed at Jan, a wistful look lingering in her eyes.

She loved her bridegroom back on Earth, Jan thought sadly.

Taddus touched his bandaged neck. "We'll be very happy together, dear." Glaring at Jan, he added, "I like *sweet, gentle* females."

"Are you looking forward to the ceremony?" Jan asked Beth.

Beth's voice was low. "Everyone's worked so hard. I just wish—I wish it could be a *real Earth-type* wedding. I had such a beautiful dress picked out…"

Jan touched Beth's shoulder. "Honey, how would you like to wear my gown?"

* * * * *

To have and to hold...
In sickness and in health...
From this day forward,
Until the next Spring Running...

Delos' arm was tight around her waist as they waited to say their vows. "And don't think we're going to part at the next Spring Running," he whispered. "I'll *never* let another male mate with you."

Jan smiled, breathing in his intoxicating scent. She knew she'd never want anyone except him.

An hour later, she nestled close to her new husband, sharing delicacies with him as they ate from the same bowls. He couldn't seem to stop touching her. His hands caressed her face, her shoulders, her thighs.

Jan drifted in a pleasant state of arousal. Other Brides were nuzzling their husbands' necks, rubbing cheeks, stroking, touching and being touched.

The music started. Some couples rose to dance. Janis was too comfortable to move. She smiled as she looked across the room. Beth's young face glowed as she danced with Taddus.

Although it was fun to have an actual wedding, Jan realized that none of the details mattered. She didn't care that she wore a plain tunic instead of satin, that there were no candles or flowers and that the cake tasted like fish. All that mattered was that she had the right bridegroom.

Delos bent to whisper in her ear, "We didn't mate enough today."

Her pussy grew wet as she imagined him thrusting into her. "Three times wasn't enough?"

"Not nearly. I want to mount you again. I want to hear you scream with pleasure."

Her lips went dry as she pictured the scene.

"I'll lick you first, though. I'll enjoy thrusting into you when your sex is slick and wet after an orgasm." He chose a morsel from a bowl and held it to her mouth. She licked the meat. Holding his gaze, she sucked his finger into her mouth, caressing it with her tongue as though it were his cock.

"Your cabin or mine?" Jan asked.

"Whichever's closer."

Raucous music filled the room.

Delos took her hand and they threaded their way through the crowd as a thousand Brides and grooms danced together, flapping their arms in The Chicken Dance.

The earlier part of the day, the Spring Running, had been all Terilian. But this wedding was all human.

Jan hoped the blending of two cultures would continue successfully. In the meantime, she had her wedding night ahead of her.

She could hardly wait.

BRIDE REBORN

Dedication

To my good friend Jim, who has patiently listened to me talk about my stories and offered excellent suggestions.

Trademarks Acknowledgement

The author acknowledges the trademarked status and trademark owners of the following wordmarks mentioned in this work of fiction:

The Little Engine That Could: Penguin Group (USA) Inc.

Chapter One

ಉ

Christmas in July.

Snow Jarrett gasped in dismay. Red and gold tinsel dripped from the walls of her new residence—Room 342 at Harbor Views Nursing Home. A chubby lit-up Santa, his mouth fixed in an inane smile, blocked the window. Next to the blaring television, a two foot high Christmas tree blinked from gold to blue to pink.

"We call this the Christmas room," the motherly aide said, maneuvering Snow's wheelchair next to Bed Two. "Isn't it cheerful?"

"Ho ho ho," Snow answered, keeping a wary eye on the senior citizen across the room. Despite her red bathrobe and cotton-fluff hair, the woman in Bed One didn't resemble Mrs. Claus as much as she did the Nutcracker.

"Let's get you settled." The aide nodded to her helper, a serene-faced black man, who drew back the bed covers and plumped the pillows.

"Nurse!" The old woman's voice was surprisingly loud. "I need help!"

"Just a minute," the female aide responded. Her helper lifted Snow out of the wheelchair and safely into bed. Snow sighed with relief.

"How old are you, honey?" the man asked. "Thirty?"

"Thirty-two," she said, watching to make sure the female aide hung her catheter bag correctly.

The man shook his head. "Damn shame."

She compressed her lips. She hated sympathy. Sympathy made her feel like crying. And she never cried, not if she could help it.

"Nurse! I need help!" The words erupted from the old woman every thirty seconds, like a dog that wouldn't stop barking.

Finally the black man walked to her side. "What d'you need, Mrs. King?"

The woman pointed at Snow. "Who's that?"

"Your new roommate."

Snow turned her head to look at Mrs. King. Even that slight movement was an effort. "Hi there. I'm Snow Jarrett."

"What kind of a name is that?"

"I was born during a blizzard." *And I've been nothing but trouble ever since.*

"You're awfully young to be here." The old woman sounded disapproving, as though Snow were a kid sneaking into an R-rated movie.

"Sorry, I didn't know there were age restrictions on terminal illness." She compressed her lips, ashamed of her sarcasm. Nothing like starting off on the wrong foot with her roomie.

Lowering her voice, she asked the female aide, "Can you please pull the curtain between the beds?"

The aide returned a sympathetic look. "If I do, she'll say she can't breathe."

"Never mind." Snow sank back against the pillows.

Primary progressive multiple sclerosis. The disease that had seized control of her body five years ago wasn't going to let up. She'd never been lucky enough to enter remission.

No complaining, she reminded herself. Her body had gone to hell and her brain had white spots all over it, but at least she could still think straight.

"I'll need help to eat dinner." She forced the humiliating words out.

"We'll tell them up at the front desk." The motherly aide patted her shoulder. "Catch you later, sweetie." Both aides left the room.

Snow closed her eyes, trying to shut out the soap opera that held her roommate enthralled.

"I'll always love you, Amanda! I know you're going blind, but I'll always be here to take care of you!"

"Oh, Blake. I know you will. I adore you!"

Grimacing, Snow rewrote the lines in her head.

I'll always love you, Snow! At least until I get tired of pushing your wheelchair around.

What about your wedding vows, Craig? In sickness and in health, remember?

I just can't do this anymore. I'm filing for divorce.

She sure hoped reincarnation existed. Next time she was reborn, she'd put her order in early. A man who'd stay, no matter what difficulties arose. Kids, two or three of them. Maybe even four. A nice house in the 'burbs.

No use dwelling on that. She ought to think about dinner. Eating was the last pleasure left to her. She could no longer see well enough to read. A "battery-operated boyfriend" used to fulfill her desires, but six months ago she'd lost the hand and arm strength needed for a vibrator.

Strange how sexual arousal lingered, even when she could no longer satisfy it. Sometimes her dreams tormented her with images of a man's muscular body covering hers, his long cock thrusting into her, making her cry out with rapture…

Until she woke, covered with sweat, blinking back tears of frustration.

She sighed, trying not to think about sex. That part of her life was over.

Her eyes fluttered shut, the fatigue she'd been fighting for the last hour overtaking her. In spite of the noisy television she fell asleep, waking only when she heard a thump.

Her dinner tray was on her bedside table, two feet out of reach. She drew a dismayed breath, her heart sinking at the prospect of hunting for the call button.

The TV squawked, making Snow wince. A deep voice blared through the room, "People of Earth. I am Primus Taddus of the Black-Striped Pelt, a Council member of the colonization ship *Ecstasy of Generations*."

Had her roommate switched to a science fiction channel?

"Necessity has compelled us to seek your help," the voice continued. "In the fourth year of our seven-year journey, a short stay on a planetary satellite exposed us to an unknown virus. To our great sorrow, every one of our females perished."

Snow squinted at the screen, her bad eyesight barely able to make out the image of a broad-shouldered man with black hair, an odd mustache and...*pointed, furry ears?*

"We require wives. A review of the populated planets in your region revealed that Earth females are the closest genetically to our species. Thus we have decided to take one thousand human females with us."

"What a horrible program!" Mrs. King exclaimed, switching the channel. But every time she pressed the remote, the same face blinked onto the screen.

"We carefully chose fertile females under age forty, childless and not presently pair-bonded. Do not be concerned for your compatriots—they will have rich and rewarding lives in a far more enlightened society than your own.

"We regret the necessity for our actions and thank you most sincerely for your time and trouble."

As the man finished speaking, Snow lost consciousness.

* * * * *

Soft gurgles moved gently across the silent space. Oxygen? IV machines? Struggling from the clutches of sleep, Snow wrinkled her nose at the unmistakable odor of antiseptic. Was she in the hospital? Wait, hadn't she just entered Harbor Views Nursing Home?

"This one's beautiful." The masculine voice close to her bed sounded enthusiastic. "Don't you agree?"

"Lovely," another voice seconded. The rumbling deepness attracted her and the sincere approval in the man's tone sent a frisson of pleasure down her spine. "Still…this doesn't change my opinion, Delos. Big mistake."

Opening her eyes to slits, Snow glimpsed the most gorgeous man she'd ever seen. His skin was a delicious creamy caramel while his eyes were an unusual golden brown. His long hair hung free, spilling over his shoulders and halfway down his chest. Despite his hair's silver shade, his face was youthful and unlined.

Emerging from the top of his head were pointed ears. She had to be dreaming. Or hallucinating.

Had she died? She'd thought angels would have wings, not furry cat ears. Gosh, maybe she'd gone to the other place.

No way. She could accept a demon with pointed ears…but not one who was breathtakingly handsome.

"Doing nothing would have been a mistake," the first voice spoke again. "Look, Ryus. Doesn't it make you feel better, seeing all these beautiful Earth females? We've got something to live for again. Our venture won't fail. And we'll have wives."

When Ryus replied, his voice went so low that Snow could barely make out his words. "*Had* a wife."

The first one—Delos?—huffed out a breath in exasperation. "We all did. But they're gone. We have to look to the future."

His voice took on a caring note. "I could help you with that. Two days in Sick Bay undergoing memory diminishment treatment...you'd still remember Arooa but the pain would lessen."

"I will never forget Arooa!" Ryus' voice boomed across the white noise. Snow's eyes opened wide.

"Snow Jarrett—you're awake. That's good." The one named Delos drew near and gave her a warm smile. "I'm your doctor, Secondus Delos of the Tawny-Spotted Pelt. How are you feeling? Any pain?"

Strange. Her eyesight seemed to have improved radically. How was that possible? Her heart pounded faster with pleasure and excitement.

She saw the doctor clearly, a slender man whose brown hair contained variegated tawny spots. His handsome friend, Ryus, hung back by the door.

Their faces were odd... Small noses, rounded eyes. Whisker-like mustaches. And those catlike ears.

The memory returned like water breaking through a levee. *We require wives...*

"You're not...not human," Snow faltered.

The doctor spoke gravely. "Correct. We're from the planet Teril."

They were aliens. Overcome by trembling, she bit her lip.

Ryus stepped forward. "Don't be afraid." He was taller than the doctor, with powerful shoulders. Although he wore a gray tunic, the musculature of his broad chest was evident. He looked like a Greek statue come to life. Zeus without a beard. Frightened though she was, she couldn't look away.

Lifting a square from the end of her bed, he shook it out until it was blanket-sized and covered her with it. Although as thin as a sheet of printer paper, it immediately surrounded her with warmth. The kindly gesture eased some of her fear.

Ryus turned to Delos, glaring. "Tranquilizer?" His tone was accusing.

"In her system already," Delos said.

So an alien ship had come to Earth, made the broadcast and taken one thousand human women. Including her.

Her shoulders shook with sudden mirth.

"Still cold?" Ryus asked, frowning.

She could no longer contain hysterical laughter. "You brought *me* here to be someone's wife? Gosh, I always thought aliens with spaceships would be *intelligent*. Don't you know I'm too weak to walk? Or even feed myself?"

Delos quirked up an eyebrow. "Are you speaking of the autoimmune disease that was destroying your myelin?"

Snow's laughter stilled. If she wasn't any use to them, what would they do with her? "I'm in the last stages of multiple sclerosis."

He smiled. "Not anymore. You're cured."

* * * * *

Arooa would have liked this Earth female. His wife had admired courage above all else.

Ryus tried to imagine being snatched from the home world, waking on a colonization ship under observation by two unfamiliar beings. A situation where his physical strength would be useless.

And yet this female had laughed at them.

Now her small face held a shocked expression. Her surprise and fright stirred him. Why was Del just standing there? Anyone could see the female needed comforting.

He drew closer then halted, the sweet scent of her body suddenly overpowering him. The Sick Bay orderlies bathed the Brides every three days. He smelled the soap they used, flavored with *hizzel* leaves. And a deeper scent as well, an enticing aroma that related to her personal essence.

Something about this female bypassed the thinking part of his brain, the part that never forgot about his dead wife. He wanted to gather the Earth woman into his arms, smooth her tumbled curls, whisper reassurance into her oddly rounded ears.

As he breathed in more of her attractive scent, an image assailed him. Snow on her knees, looking back at him with a smile. Waiting eagerly for him to mount her. Craving the deep plunge of his engorged organ.

Delos noticed his hesitation. "Was I right?" the doctor asked softly.

Ryus replied with an irritated growl. He was determined to resist the anti-erection patch Del had offered earlier that day. Why would he need such a thing? He wasn't going to let his organ's demands overcome his moral objections, like the rest of them had. He could control himself.

Stealing the Earth women was *wrong*.

He put his hand on Snow's shoulder, the only part of her body that wasn't covered. "Strive for calm, little one. No one will hurt you. Promise."

She snatched his hand and held it to her cheek. He drew a shocked breath, his groin tightening.

Tears welled in her large gray eyes. Her fingers trembled around his.

"I'm *cured*? I can't believe it! How—how did that happen?"

Ryus jerked his head toward Del. "His idea."

She stared at the doctor, whispering, "Thank you. *Thank you.*"

Ryus shifted uneasily. Not only had he been against stealing the Earth women, he'd argued in the all-ship meeting that if they *had* to do it, only healthy Brides should be brought aboard.

But Del's enthusiasm and assurances had carried the day. And he wasn't even a primus.

"It wasn't difficult." Delos smoothed a nonexistent wrinkle in his blue tunic. "We estimate our culture is two or three hundred years ahead of Earth's technology. I simply altered our cure for a similar disease to fit your human physiology."

"You can't imagine what this means to me." Her enchantingly husky voice deepened slightly. "It's an incredible gift."

"Not a gift," Ryus warned. "Payment expected."

She blinked up at him. "What—oh, you mean the wife part." She looked to Delos and back to him. "How bad could it be?"

Her gaze held him like a *patitou* caught in a snare. Sweat broke out on his forehead. What was it about her? If Del hadn't been in the room, he'd have sat on the side of her bed and stared into those lovely eyes, breathing in her wonderful scent. Listened to her speak, acquainting himself with her essence. Stroked her rounded breasts…*no*.

"You'll be fine," Delos reassured her. "No need to worry about marriage now. You have plenty of time. In fact, you're the first Bride I've awakened."

"Why me?"

"You need extra time to get stronger. Your disease is gone, but the muscular weakness remains. I've made improvements, but some of it will be up to you. That's where Ryus comes in."

Ryus tapped his right shoulder in agreement. Then realizing this human didn't understand the gesture's meaning, he said, "Physical therapist. I'll help you." He fought a rush of anticipation.

Her soft fingers squeezed his. "I look forward to working with you."

Solange Ayre

* * * * *

Snow lay with closed eyes, trying to make sense of everything the two Terilians had told her.

She ought to be angry at the mass kidnapping. She regretted the objections sure to come from the other women but she couldn't think about that now. She was *healthy*. She wasn't going to die at the nursing home. What an incredible second chance.

She would have a husband.

What were Terilian husbands like?

If the doctor and the physical therapist were representative of their kind, she had nothing to worry about. Perhaps even something to anticipate.

Shivering, she once again experienced the thrill that had zipped through her body when Ryus touched her. And how wonderful the two males had smelled. Delos' scent reminded her of chocolate but Ryus possessed the enticing aroma of fresh mint. She used to pick mint leaves in her mother's garden and bring them inside to serve with iced tea. The happy memory made her smile.

Ryus would be her physical therapist. Warmth flooded her as she thought of him helping her move her limbs and guiding her first attempts at walking.

A twinge of arousal had her hand moving to her mound. The motion was effortless. It was true — whatever the doctor had done had made her much stronger.

Would she be able to move her legs? Before she'd even completed the thought, she parted them. Exhilaration raced through her and she let out a whoop of triumph.

Thank you, Dr. Delos.

But it wasn't Delos who wouldn't leave her thoughts. It was Ryus.

How gentle he'd been when he covered her with the blanket. She couldn't clear his tantalizing image from her mind. And what fascinating eyes he had, so intelligent and alert…and yet sorrow lingered in his gaze.

Did he ever smile?

Would he ever smile at *her*?

She stroked her damp curls, wondering how Terilians made love. Would Ryus know how to tease her nipples until they peaked? How to rub her clit in a gentle yet stimulating way?

Moisture drenched her pussy as she slid a finger inside. She imagined Ryus in bed with her, kissing her neck, sucking her nipples.

What did he look like under that concealing tunic? How was his cock shaped? What positions did he prefer for sex?

Her hand moved faster, thrumming quickly and lightly over her clit. Her breathing quickened.

She pictured his extraordinary golden-brown eyes gazing down at her as he thrust deeply inside her body. His powerful cock filling her, pleasuring every nerve.

Weakly, her pelvis throbbed with a short, quick climax.

Okay, she'd had better.

But it felt darned wonderful after six weary months without one.

* * * * *

The next morning, Ryus joined Delos in the doctor's office after Second Meal. The doctor sat frowning at his computer interface.

"How is Snow today?" Ryus asked.

"Vital signs are excellent this morning. Also I'm pleased to say she masturbated after we left yesterday."

Ryus didn't understand why this plain statement of fact sent arousal surging through him. "Impressive." He strove for a detached tone. "Shows resilience."

Delos grinned. "Or it shows your pheromones were affecting her."

"You were there too," Ryus answered dryly.

"She was staring at you, not me."

"She was curious. Never seen Terilians before." If Delos was implying something more, Ryus didn't want to think about it.

Delos shoved an anti-erection patch across the desk. "Wear this today."

Remembering his nearly uncontrollable reaction when he'd met the Earth female the day before, Ryus slapped the patch on his bare shoulder without comment.

"Well, she's all yours. The equipment you ordered is in her cabin." Delos got up to leave. "Contact me with any problems."

Ryus stared at him. "Where are *you* going?"

"To check on Janis Stone."

Ryus pictured the beautiful female Delos had pointed out to him yesterday when he'd accompanied the doctor on his daily rounds among the Brides. He eyed his friend sympathetically. Del's comments verified what he'd suspected the day before.

"Fifty primuses aboard," Ryus warned him. "One's bound to claim her. Council member, probably."

"She's my patient. Nothing more."

Despite the disclaimer, the doctor was quivering with eagerness to leave. A mere two years and his deceased wife Bashia was the last thing on his mind.

Well, Bashia had certainly not been Arooa's equal. No other female was.

Or ever would be.

Chapter Two

Stretching, Snow basked in the heat of the overhead lamps like a cat enjoying the sunlight.

Dr. Delos had come by earlier. How kind he'd been, answering her many questions, helping her with breakfast. Still, she couldn't avoid a twinge of disappointment. The doctor had been her only visitor.

"Is Ryus busy today?" she'd asked finally.

Was there a knowing gleam in the doctor's eyes? "You'll see him soon."

Snow fingered the fabric of her tunic. Deep rose, as soft as satin, it made her feel attractive. Quite a contrast to the hospital gowns she'd lived in for the past few years.

The tunic was surprisingly sheer, revealing her nipples and the dark curls between her thighs. Dr. Delos had assured her it was customary apparel for Terilian females.

But perhaps he was part of a male conspiracy, the equivalent of naïve women being told by human men, *It's customary to wear thongs and pasties.*

She giggled at the thought. And stopped abruptly when the door slid open and Ryus walked in.

Her eyes widened. During the night, she'd decided he couldn't possibly be as handsome as she'd thought at first. But she'd been wrong. He was *more* attractive than she remembered. Arousal shivered through her, filling her pussy with warmth.

Why was she so excited by his presence? He wasn't even human!

The corners of his beautifully cut mouth lifted. At last, a smile.

"Happy today?" he asked.

"You bet. Any place would be better than—" she hesitated. She was fluent in the Terilian language, due to the computer chip Dr. Delos had installed, but she didn't seem to know a term for *nursing home*.

"You were in a perpetual-care hospital." She must have shown her surprise, for he added, "Saw your files."

"I expected to die there," Snow said. "So this is fine by me—I've always danced to a different drummer. But I'll bet the other women won't have the same reaction."

Unlike his silvery hair, his eyebrows were dark. They arched upward as he asked, "They will resist?"

"How the heck should I know? I can tell you one thing, they aren't going to be happy. How would you like to leave everything you'd ever known and your family—"

"We have," he interrupted. "All of us are colonists. We'll never return to our home world."

"But *you* left voluntarily," she shot back. "You weren't *kidnapped*."

He flinched and his brows drew together. Turning away, he opened a drawer built into the wall. She had time to study his muscular shoulders and wide back.

Why did she keep hoping he would come closer? She wanted to run her hands through his long hair, caress his shoulders, lick him...

Lick him? Where had that come from?

"Kidnapped," he said. "Ugly word."

"Ugly word—ugly crime."

He stalked toward her, long white cords dangling from his hands. Electrical wires? Had it all been a lie? Would she be tortured instead of wedded?

The wall monitor behind her chirped, drawing Ryus' attention. "What's wrong?" He sounded genuinely puzzled. "Pulse spiked."

She put her hand to her galloping heart. "What are those cords?"

"Electronic crutches." He frowned. "Did you think I would *hurt* you?"

"Well…I don't know you." She felt a little ashamed of her momentary terror. So far, he'd been nothing but kind.

"Yesterday. Made you a promise."

She remembered every word he'd said. "You promised no one would hurt me."

"Remember that." His deep voice vibrated with sincerity. Although she had no reason for trust, she believed him.

He came to the side of her bed and held up the cords. "Calibrated for your particular structure. Support your muscles, stimulate the nerves. Ready to walk?"

"*Today*?" Surely he was joking.

"Today," he answered firmly. "Straighten and part your legs." He picked up the bedcover, ready to whisk it away.

She hesitated, embarrassed by the way her tunic revealed her body. And she certainly didn't want him to see her legs. A big male like him probably wanted a statuesque Bride with long, slender legs.

"Now what's wrong?" He had every right to be impatient with her, but his voice was gentle.

"I'm…I'm not used to all this." Her cheeks heated as he pulled the cover away, exposing her weak, helpless legs.

"Here to help you." He laid one cord down and straightened the other.

How many physicians had poked and prodded her over the last five years? He was just like a doctor…with furry ears.

But it didn't do any good to tell herself that. No doctor had ever had such a wonderful scent, that subtle mint that made her want to explore every inch of his muscular body. Had she ever been so aware of a male's personal scent before?

The skirt of her tunic reached to her knees. He drew it back, raising it to just below her mound.

She noticed the hitch in his breath. Was he shocked by her figure? He must be wondering why his people had chosen a woman who was not only ill but overweight.

He laid the cord along her right leg, his fingers tickling her thighs. She shivered under his touch, a teasing ache stirring deep inside her.

The cord adhered to her inner thigh, although she felt no stickiness. A heady tingling ran up and down her muscles.

For the last three years, her legs had been like nearly inert blobs, as though they weren't even part of her. Now they felt alive again. What a fantastic sensation.

She gulped. Was it possibly true? Would she really be able to walk today?

He attached the other cord, his warm palms moving slowly down her thigh. Was this a medically necessary touch? Or a caress? Surely his breathing had quickened.

She gazed up at his face questioningly. Their eyes met. He jerked back as though her body had seared him. No doubt he was relieved to be done with her.

"Soon you'll be strong enough to attach the crutches yourself." He raked his hair back from his face. "Good thing. Trying to be professional, but…have to realize, we've been without mates for two years. Your loveliness is hard to withstand."

"My what?"

"Can't keep talking about it. Your scent alone…overwhelming." Frowning, he stepped back a few paces. "Bed!" he commanded. "Raise patient, one hundred twenty degree angle."

Slowly the bed tilted upward, bringing her to a sitting position.

Her scent overwhelmed him? As much as his scent enticed her?

"Shoes," he muttered. He found them in a drawer, flexible shoes resembling slippers. They were an exact match for her rose tunic. He drew them over her feet with infinite care, as though handling a fragile porcelain vase.

What would he be like in bed? Would he be solely concerned with his own pleasure? Or would he use that gentle touch to bring a lover to ecstasy? To bring *her* to ecstasy?

He reached for her. "Give me your hands."

She laid them in his palms. Hers looked like a child's, dwarfed by his. Gosh, he could crack open concrete with those big hands.

She sensed his strength as he helped her turn on the bed so that her legs dangled off the side. At Ryus' command, the bed lowered until her feet touched the floor.

"Good," he said. "Now stand."

Despite the warmth of the room, she shivered. "I-I don't think I can."

"Secondus Delos is an excellent doctor." He tightened his grip. "Says you're ready."

"But I haven't stood in three years!" Terror dried her mouth.

"Try. I'll help."

Come on, girl! Don't be the "little engine that couldn't". In spite of the warm clasp of his hands, her arms shook.

Or worse yet, "the little engine that wouldn't even try".

Gritting her teeth, she shifted her weight to her feet. Electrical impulses chased each other up and down her legs, a sensation both strange and pleasurable. Ryus pulled gently and steadily on her arms, helping her rise.

She stood.

Her head swam and her legs trembled. But triumph exploded inside her like Fourth of July fireworks. "I did it!" she gasped.

"Knew you could." His pleased expression was the perfect counterpart to her own excitement. The eager light in his eyes thrilled her. Gosh, he looked so different when he smiled. Younger, less forbidding.

He stepped back, his long arms extended. "Come to me."

Did she remember how to walk? Once she'd been able to run and jump effortlessly. Could she ever regain those skills?

First one leg, then the other. That shift from foot to foot — that was the hard part. As complex as a dance step.

But she was doing it. She drew closer, closer...then something went wrong and she stumbled.

He caught her in his arms, steadying her against his broad chest. Delicious, solid muscle. His warm embrace felt oh-so good, as though she'd known him for years as a trusted friend.

He stepped back before she had time to revel in his closeness. "Doing great. And don't worry about falling. The crutches project a gravity field. You *can't* fall."

Reassured, she practiced walking around the small room, clinging to Ryus' arm.

Once she felt steadier, she broke the silence by asking, "How long have you been a physical therapist?"

"Since I was sixteen. Fourteen years."

He was only thirty years old? His commanding presence had made her think he was older.

"You were a teacher on Earth," he said. "Enjoy it?"

"I taught American History at Northcoast University. But what I really liked was research and writing." She sighed, thinking of her meticulously detailed nonfiction book, *Uncharted Lands: A History of the Western Reserve.* No book signings for her. By the time it had been published, she was housebound.

"Maybe that's why you were chosen, aside from your beauty," Ryus said. "The historians who were documenting our great colonization venture are dead. Council may ask you to continue their work."

She glowed inside at the idea of doing something useful again. Too much of her life on Earth had dragged by the last few years while she lay bored and helpless, praying only for death.

"I'll have to learn to read and write your language." She wondered how long it would take. She hoped the Terilians had a simple alphabet, like English, rather than thousands of characters, like Chinese.

The corners of his sensual mouth rose. "Already know it," he told her. "Brain chip gives you written language as well as speech."

She drew an excited breath. She hadn't been able to hold a book for the last eight months. "Oh, it'll be wonderful to read and study again!"

"Ship's computer contains most Terilian books of the Modern Era. Bring you a computer interface soon."

"When can I have it? Tomorrow? Today?"

He smiled, his golden eyes teasing her. *"Soon,"* he repeated. "Concentrate on physical therapy first."

She kept walking. After a half hour, she felt exhausted yet exhilarated at the same time. And here she'd been ready to cock up her toes. Not by a long shot!

Ryus admired the female's persistence. Over the years, many of his clients had had to be coaxed to do their exercises, like youths who refused to study. Others started with good intentions but gave up quickly when they tired. Snow kept pushing herself.

She was not only beautiful and intelligent but brave as well.

Not that it mattered to him.

He thought of the desolate asteroid where they'd left their dead. A good portion of the males. All the young. All the wives. He'd considered staying with Arooa, slashing his throat with his claws in the Old Tradition. Only the thought of how angry she'd have been kept him from doing it.

Snow's hand trembled on his arm.

Pay attention to your patient. "Break," he told her.

"I want to keep working." She spoke through gritted teeth.

"Not asking." He led her to the bed. She gave in and sat, panting with the effort she'd made. "Riharyazz wasn't built in a day," he quoted the old proverb.

"Where…is…that?" She wiped her forehead.

"Eastern hemisphere of Teril." She was too exhausted to converse, so he kept talking. "Ancient city built in the tallest trees on the planet. *Big* trees. Trunk circumferences of over a mile. Branches twice as wide as this room."

"I wish I could see it," she said wistfully.

He lowered his hand to her shoulder. "Lie down. Time for a massage."

She looked startled but pleased. "Oh! That's very kind of you."

"Therapy. Another way to stimulate your muscles." He helped her lift her legs onto the bed, touched by the trusting look she gave him.

"Should I roll over?"

"Stay like that." As soon as the words were out of his mouth, he regretted them. It would have been easier to massage her legs without looking at the pretty nipples peeping coyly through her tunic.

On the other hand, massaging her sensuously curved buttocks would have reminded him of mating. Was there anything better than the heady aroma of an aroused female, quivering as she waited to be mounted?

Why wasn't that patch working? He hadn't expected Del's medicine to be so ineffective.

Clearly the patch had been overcome by this Earth female's incredibly powerful pheromones.

Her soft white thighs were proving to be a wickedly pleasurable temptation. For the last two years, his clients had been males with arm or leg strains from exercising or mock-fighting. Massaging a female again was a pleasant contrast. A female smelled so much better, felt so much better. Her voice pleased his ears…

"Tell me more about Riharyazz," she said. "Have you been there?"

"Visited with my wife. The first time we married." He'd made his way down to her dimpled knee. She uttered a sound of pleasure as he worked the muscles.

Like a female's passionate cry when a male enters her.

"What do you mean, the first time you married?" she asked.

He frowned, trying to remember what he'd read about Earthian customs. "That's right, your people vow to stay together for life. Terilians don't. Couples without young participate every five years in the Spring Running. Choose another mate, or choose each other again. Arooa and I chose each other three times."

He massaged the pale flesh of her calves then moved down to her shapely ankles. Gently he removed her shoes. A mistake, for he immediately found himself captivated by her delicate pink toes.

The room was suddenly much too warm. Would she notice he was sweating? If she did, hopefully she would think it was due to his physical efforts rather than the arousal threatening to pull him under.

He had to think of a neutral topic. Nothing about marriage…or mating…

"What's the Spring Running?" she asked.

A sudden vision unfolded of Snow healthy enough to run, fleeing from him, dodging in between trees yet watching to make sure he didn't lose sight of her—the way females always did at the Running. And the glorious moment when he'd catch her, bury his face in her black curls and lick the tender back of her neck. She'd spread her legs, her labia swollen and slick, wanton and eager as he thrust into her from behind.

"Mating ritual." His organ rose, straining against his tights. "Talk about something else."

Her expression revealed surprise at his abrupt tone. "I've been wondering about the illness," she said. "Was it only the wives who became sick?"

The topic dampened his desire. He was able to massage her ankles and push the intrusive thoughts aside.

"Everyone was sick. Three hundred and four adult males died. Females and young most susceptible. Del has theories...ask him."

She drew in a shocked breath. "Young? You mean—"

"All offspring died." He and Arooa hadn't been able to have young but he'd been fond of Arooa's sister's offspring, particularly little Otirus. He closed his eyes, shutting out the image of the young male's mischievous face.

"It's a wonder you people were able to go on." Her voice trembled as though she actually understood what they'd endured. Who would have thought an Earth woman would have so much compassion for the people who had stolen her away?

He wanted to pull her close and thank her for her kindness. "Some of us...some of us wanted to die...with the others."

"I can imagine." She threaded her fingers together. "When my husband left me—at first I didn't know how I'd go on. My friends rallied around to help me through. It's hard to think what would have happened if all of us had lost spouses at the same time."

"Husband left you? Why?" Had the human suffered from a brain illness? Why would any male leave such an enticing female?

"I don't think he ever truly loved me." Her voice dropped low, but not so low that he couldn't hear the pain in it. "He turned to me after his long-time girlfriend broke up with him. I was always second best for him."

His heart overturned. What a thoughtless, dishonorable person the Earthian male must have been.

He laid her foot down. The urgent need to release his claws was overpowering. "Wish he was here. Needs a lesson in being a good husband." His claws shot forward, pearly gray, two inches long, sharp enough to score metal. He craved a word of admiration on their length and lethal appearance.

She gasped. "What are those? *Claws*?" Her wide eyes and quivering chin revealed her fright.

She was from Earth. Naturally she didn't understand yet about the Weapons of Valor. He forced himself to retract them.

"You'll have claws too." He spoke in his most reassuring tone. "You're growing them as part of the Transition. You'll also gain an enhanced sense of smell, enhanced hearing and greater strength."

"I've noticed the enhanced sense of smell." She held her hands up in front of her face, looking at her feeble Earthian fingernails. "But *claws*? I'm not sure I want them."

"*Must* have claws." How could anyone reject this great gift? "Only criminals lack them."

"What happens to them?"

"Surgical removal. Partly punishment, partly so they can't hurt anyone."

A shudder passed through her. "There's so much to get used to here." She compressed her lips, then went on, "But it's worth it. Everything's worth it to get my strength and mobility back. It's like being reborn."

"Glad you feel that way." How he wished to be reborn, without the grief that was like a claw embedded in his heart.

The door chimed. A moment later an orderly entered with a tray. "Secondus Delos says I'm to stay and help the female eat Third Meal."

Snow raised herself on her elbows, her gaze devouring the handsome young male. Not surprising, since he was only the third Terilian she'd seen. Yet Ryus hated her interest.

The orderly's gaze lingered on Snow's breasts.

"Take good care of this female," Ryus said. "Don't do anything to frighten her." He added a quick growl for emphasis.

The orderly backed away, intimidated. "Yes, Primus." The bowls he carried clattered against the tray.

"More food?" Snow raised her brows. "I'll gain weight if I keep eating like this."

"Hope so." Ryus caught his breath. Her beauty would be incredibly enhanced by more padding on her breasts and hips.

She gave him a wondering look. "Men back home thought I was too heavy."

"Earthian culture showed many signs of serious dysfunction." He went to the door. "Nap after eating—customary following Third Meal."

"Wait! Will I see you later?"

The longing in her voice made his heart clench. "Tomorrow. Promise."

* * * * *

Snow spent the next day eagerly awaiting Ryus' arrival. She had no doubt he would return. Somehow she felt certain that he always kept his word.

He entered her cabin after Fourth Meal, which had been a delicious spicy drink accompanied by crunchy sticks. After greeting her, Ryus held up a small electronic screen. "Del says, time to test your orgasmic strength."

"*What?* Why do you need to know that?"

"For the medical records," he replied evasively.

"You're going to test me with *that*?" Snow touched the edge of the square device. It didn't look like any vibrator she'd ever seen.

"Machine records the measurement. Also can provide electronic nerve stimulation by remote control—one method." He gave her an uneasy look. "Second method—autostimulation."

"Masturbation, you mean? While you *watch*?" She frowned at him. "No way! What are my other options?"

"Manual stimulation by a partner."

Now this was getting interesting. "By you?"

He hesitated. "If that's your preferred method."

"Are you saying you'll give me an orgasm and take no pleasure for yourself?"

"Just more physical therapy. Taking medication to control sexual urges."

Snow sat back, reflecting on his offer. She certainly didn't like the first two choices. Receiving an orgasm by remote control would make her feel like a puppet. And masturbation was a private matter.

Besides, how bad could it be, to have this incredibly sexy male touching her, caressing her, making her come?

"All right, manual stimulation it is," she said. As he pulled a stool next to the bed, she added, "Won't you lie down with me?"

He froze. "Is that a requirement?"

"If you want me to cooperate, that's part of the deal." She moved over on the bed, leaving him room to join her. "And take your clothes off."

His brows came together. "Why?"

She huffed with exasperation. "Because if we're going to do something sexual, we're both getting naked. Don't Terilians undress when they have sex?"

"Usually. Unless the need is urgent."

Urgent…now there was an enticing thought. She imagined him discarding his businesslike manner, coming to her and jerking aside her tunic with overwhelming desire. Her hips shifted restlessly.

Doubt flitted over his expression. Then resignation. Finally he made an adjustment to the machine he held and laid it on the stool.

Grasping his tunic, he lifted it over his head.

She would be the first Earth woman to see a Terilian naked. Anticipation rose in her, gale force.

His chest was gorgeous. Devoid of hair, it was broad and rippling with well-defined musculature. She wanted to run her palms over his skin, kiss his dark nipples, lick every inch of him.

"Turn around," she commanded.

He obeyed. His long hair was pulled back into a ponytail. There was something odd about his back…

"Move your hair aside," she said. With a brush of his hand, he shifted his ponytail to the front, revealing a three-inch swath of silver hair running down his back and into his tights. Or perhaps it was more like fur, since it looked soft and velvety. How would it feel if she stroked it?

"Do all of you have hair on your backs?" she asked.

"We all have pelts, yes."

Her gaze dropped to his muscular buttocks, barely concealed by his clinging gray tights. "Remove your tights too," she said, keeping her tone relentless.

"Unnecessary," he protested.

"If I'm going to marry here on the ship, I need to see what you males look like." After all, wasn't this crucial? What if their alien anatomy wasn't a good fit with human anatomy?

Surely they'd checked that out beforehand.

Ryus hooked his hands into the waistband of his tights. Suppose Terilians had pencil-thin penises? She gulped in dismay.

He pulled his tights down.

Jackpot!

His cock was beautiful. The perfect size, long enough to be exciting to view, thick enough that her small hand wouldn't quite close around it. The head was oddly shaped, more like a long cylinder than a human male's mushroom shape.

She wondered what his organ would look like erect. Did Terilian males even *get* erections, like humans? How would he respond if she cradled his cock in her palm, slowly stroked him from the head all the way to his heavy testicles?

She looked up into his golden eyes and found him watching her with amusement. "Curiosity satisfied?" he asked.

Satisfied? I won't be satisfied until you're thrusting inside me.

Shocked at the wanton thought, she looked away. *Manual stimulation* was what he'd promised to provide. Nothing more.

"Help me with my clothing." She raised her arms.

Carefully he pulled her tunic over her head. His hands brushed against her full breasts. She quivered and her nipples peaked instantly. How she longed for a firmer, deliberate touch.

His eyes lingered on her naked breasts. She sat back, shaken by the way his hungry gaze affected her.

He turned his head. "Forgive me," he muttered.

"Why do you say that?" After all, she was the one who'd chosen door number three.

"Trying to keep this impersonal."

"Don't." She patted the place beside her. "Come sit with me."

He eased onto the bed. This close, his scent flooded her senses. She caught her breath. After years of nothing but impersonal caregiving from nurses and aides, she was starved for a sexual touch. She couldn't wait for him to caress her.

Would he kiss her? She imagined the wet stroke of his tongue against hers, the feel of his hands pulling her close against his chest.

She wanted those hands on her breasts again.

They looked at each other for a long moment. His golden brown eyes were beautiful. Their elongated pupils had seemed strange at first, but she was already growing used to them.

Putting his hand on her upper thigh, he said, "Open your legs."

His light touch entranced her, made her want to lie back and do exactly as he'd said. But it wouldn't be enough. She had to be strong.

She forced herself to push his fingers aside. "I don't know what your females were like, but Earth women need romance. You want me to have an orgasm? Then act like a lover, not a scientist."

His brows drew down angrily. Then his expression shifted to consternation. "Not easy for me."

"What's that supposed to mean?" When he didn't answer, she went on, "I thought this whole kidnapping caper was because you Terilians need wives."

He met her gaze squarely. "Still feel married."

She fell silent, struck by his devotion. What human man loved his wife so deeply that he still felt married, two years after her death?

"Does that mean you're *not* going to marry an Earth woman?" The possibility troubled her.

He grimaced. "Told the Council they were immoral to steal you humans. Should I participate in something I believe is wrong?"

"Maybe not," she answered reluctantly. Her heart sank. Somehow she'd been thinking maybe he would marry *her*. "But it's moot now. We're here. So maybe you *should* participate."

He didn't reply but his expression showed his inner turmoil.

"Do you have any other options?" she asked.

"Wait until we get to the new planet. Might be a female there for me. Someone who's lost her husband to death." He hesitated. "Del says another year without mating will kill us. Our bodies need release. Only way is by mating. Males can't climax through masturbation."

The idea was shocking—a whole world of males who *couldn't jack off*.

"So you don't have a choice," she said. "This goes beyond a moral principle. It's life or death for you."

"That's what Del *says*. Think he's wrong. Think I can handle it."

A typical male, believing a doctor's pronouncement didn't apply to *him*. She wanted to yell at him, to demand he listen to what the doctor told him.

But there were some males who couldn't be told a darn thing. Her ex-husband came to mind. Ryus was probably even more stubborn. She restrained herself from demanding, *Are you nuts*?

A softer approach was necessary. "Well," she said lightly, "even if you don't want to marry again, *I* certainly plan on it. So I'd appreciate it if you'd show me what to expect from a Terilian husband." She instructed the bed to lower the back and settled herself into a comfortable position.

"All right." He laced his fingers together and flexed them, his expression revealing some doubt. "We'll start with your legs."

Her legs? Well, maybe it helped if he told himself it was therapy. Remembering how wonderful his massage had felt yesterday, she had no objections.

Turning, he lay on his side facing her, his head near her feet. He rubbed her ankles, his strong fingers making small circles. "Ankles are two of the five hundred and forty-four pleasure points on the female body — at least for Terilians. Like it?"

Her breath expelled on a sigh. "*Very* much." Two down, five hundred and forty-two more pleasure points to go. She couldn't wait.

She'd never realized her ankles were erogenous zones. His stroking and rubbing swiftly built heat inside her.

Cradling her foot in one hand, he brought her toes to his mouth. "Tempted to do this earlier." He took her big toe into his mouth and sucked.

"Oh!" she exclaimed, taken by surprise. A throbbing ache built in her pussy as he laved and sucked her toes. His mouth was warm and demanding, his tongue slightly rough, like sand on the beach. When it teased between her toes, pleasure shuddered up and down her spine. She moaned.

Shifting on the bed, he licked her knee, his tongue caressing her as though he'd never tasted anything so delicious. She quivered, overwhelmed by sensation as his mouth explored her kneecap and his tongue darted into the crevice behind her knee.

"That feels wonderful," she gasped. Already her pussy was swollen and wet. Urgency built through every limb, centering in her pelvis.

His hand settled over her mound, his fingers brushing through her tight curls. "Yes, there," she pleaded, raising her legs and parting them.

She scented the hot, sweet aroma of her own arousal. Did he notice as well? He must have, for he hesitated a moment. His breathing grew labored as his fingers gently traced her nether lips.

She'd forgotten how wonderful it felt to have a masculine hand on her, big fingers caressing, drawing forth a delicious liquid heat.

"Very responsive," he said, a note of surprise in his voice.

"Why not?" The words emerged on a gasp. It was difficult to talk when his touch gave her such extreme pleasure.

"Because you're human, I'm Terilian." He ran his tongue over his lips.

"Even so, it seems like you know how to touch a woman."

He smiled. As if to prove the truth of her words, he stroked upward, his hand brushing against her clit. Sensation rushed through her. A cry of mingled satisfaction and anticipation broke from her throat, a wordless, primitive sound.

Had she shocked him? But his smile widened. He caressed her again, another long stroke ending with more wonderful titillation of her clit. She arched her hips, trying to reach increased contact, a deeper touch.

He picked up the pace. The pleasure intensified in great ragged jolts, oscillating out of control. She rubbed against his hand, moaning and panting. "Please, Ryus." Words tumbled from her. "More—yes—touch me! Yes! Like that! Oh, please, *more*."

"Like this?" The excitement in his voice drove her arousal higher. His finger slid inside her tight channel, eased by her wetness. She arched her back, holding her breath. An orgasm rippled through her.

Her eyes fluttered closed as she reveled in the quivers chasing each other through her pussy.

Sighing, he dropped onto his back.

She opened her eyes, looking at him with gratitude. His forehead was beaded with sweat. He raised his fingers to his face, inhaling her scent like a connoisseur noting the bouquet of a fine wine.

Her earlier question was answered—yes, Terilians got erections. Large ones, judging by Ryus. His cock lay dark and engorged against his flat stomach. She gazed hungrily at it, wondering what he would do if she stroked him.

Reaching out, she caressed the length of his cock, from its thick base all the way up to the cylindrical head. His smooth skin was hot beneath her palm.

He gasped. His face twisted, his expression agonized. For a moment she was afraid she'd hurt him.

He rose out of bed in one fluid motion. Snatching his tunic, he yanked it over his head.

"What's wrong?" she asked. Was there some taboo against females touching males? Why hadn't he warned her?

"Nothing's wrong." He pulled on his tights. "Del will talk to you about your readings."

"My *readings*! Is that all you care about?"

He stalked to the door, the screen-device in his hand, his face a stern mask.

Snow sank back on the bed, feeling like she'd just been with a one-night stand who was never going to call her.

Chapter Three

ಐ

Ryus didn't take the elevator to the fourteenth floor. Instead he worked off some of his turmoil by jumping from platform to platform. Sixteen jumps brought him from the Tenth Level—Sick Bay—to the Fourteenth—Agriculture. His favorite part of the ship.

He stood for several minutes breathing deeply, drinking in the aromas of plants and soil and fresh water. In the distance, giant sprinklers walked among the crops, watering the plants that were a major food source for everyone on the ship.

His lack of control dismayed him. A few minutes touching the Earth female and he'd been ready to mate with her. Ready? No, eager. *Desperate*. He'd craved her the way a drowning person craved air.

Sickened by his disloyalty to his wife, he headed for the park. He stopped long enough to pick a few flowering *ritilla*, then headed toward the cave he and Arooa had found, early in the voyage.

The *patitou* was asleep in her cage. As he drew near, she woke and began to run in circles. "Ryus!" she squeaked. "Ryus! Food? Play?"

He couldn't help smiling at the tiny furball's antics. He lifted the cage door and put Popo on his shoulder. She snuggled against his neck, her skinny tail tickling the side of his face. Stroking her round, velvety ears, he fed her a *ritilla*.

With Arooa, he'd always pretended to dislike the little creature. "It's useless," he'd scoff. "And it stinks."

"She's loving and affectionate." Arooa had always defended Popo. She'd had the tiny pet since she was three years old and wasn't about to leave Teril without her. Since pets weren't allowed on the *Ecstasy of Generations*, it had taken a hefty bribe to the purser to get Popo aboard and a long search until Arooa had found this hiding place.

He sank down on the cold floor of the cave, letting the *patitou* scurry up and down his arm.

Suddenly she stopped and looked up at him, her beady red eyes glittering. "Rooa?" she asked. "Rooa?"

He drew in a shaky breath. "Maybe next time." *Patitous* didn't understand about death.

Neither did he.

How could he have lain with another female and touched her the way he used to touch his wife? He'd enjoyed every second too. Satisfaction had filled him when Snow cried out with passion, when his hands brought her to climax.

And his own body had responded to her. In spite of Del's drugs, in spite of the fact that she was an alien, a primitive woman from Earth...

A beautiful, enticing woman from Earth. A female he wanted to take as his mate.

"Belmarra!"

"Yes, Primus Ryus." The computer's disembodied voice echoed through the cave.

"Run Arooa program."

A moment passed. Sweet agony swept through him. He closed his eyes.

"Ryus?" Arooa's own soft voice, replicated by the program.

"Miss you," he whispered.

"We'll be together again someday," the answer came. "In the land of the Great Fur-Mother."

He didn't believe in the Old Religion but it had comforted Arooa in her last hours. "Hard to go on without you," he said.

"You must."

All words she had spoken during her life. Oh, he knew very well it was just the computer program rearranging her sentences to craft replies. Yet he could almost believe she was there.

He should be strong enough not to need this.

He wasn't.

"Your little Popo is healthy."

"That's good. She's my favorite *little* creature." Her merry giggle. "And you're my favorite *big* creature, Ry."

"Glad I'm a creature," he said, as always.

"You're the handsomest creature on the ship. I'm surprised the other wives can keep their hands off you."

He remembered the look she used to give him. The look that said, *Take me in your arms. Thrust into me until I shriek with pleasure.* A signal for him to clasp her in his arms and jump to the bed.

"Working with a new patient now. May have to do things that…that I wouldn't do if you were still here."

Did her answer take a little longer than usual? "It's wonderful how you care about your patients. I love you for that."

He sighed. "Belmarra, close Arooa program." Nothing about it was satisfying. Not any longer. Just a voice lacking scent, lacking a warm body or a gentle touch.

Nothing was the same since he'd met Snow.

He would never open the Arooa program again.

* * * * *

Bad news often arrived with breakfast, in Snow's estimation. That's when doctors made their rounds. That's when they said things like, *primary progressive multiple sclerosis. Prognosis is not good.*

Doctor Delos was no exception. His expression betrayed that she wouldn't like what he had to say. Ryus, coming in behind him, looked somber as well. But then, he usually did.

Delos pulled up a stool beside the bed. "From the information I've uplinked from your planet, I understand that Earthian sexuality is somewhat different from Terilian sexuality. Human males can masturbate. They can also mate and ejaculate even when the female fails to climax." He raised his eyebrows as though the concept surprised him. "A Terilian male can ejaculate *only* when his mate has a powerful orgasm."

"That's interesting," Snow said, trying to speak politely, but her mind was whirling. What an incentive for a male to be a great lover.

Delos frowned.

Bad news ahead. She braced herself.

"Currently your orgasmic contractions aren't strong enough to make a Terilian male ejaculate," the doctor said.

"So what are you going to do? Open an airlock and push me out?"

Delos looked shocked. "That would kill you!"

"If I can't be a Bride, what use am I to you people?"

"You *will* be a Bride." Delos patted her knee. "It's just like the walking you've been doing. You need physical therapy to build your muscles...*all* your muscles." He looked at Ryus. "Will you help Snow? She requires more intensive therapy."

Ryus' honey golden eyes battled Delos' for a long moment. Then he turned to Snow. Although he said nothing, she felt as though he were examining every part of her—her face, her breasts, her legs—maybe even the thoughts in her head.

She gazed back at him imploringly. *Please. Won't you be the one to help me?*

At last he tapped his shoulder with one hand. She was relieved—he'd agreed.

Delos smiled with satisfaction. "In my professional opinion, we need to address the situation with a two-part solution. Part one, exercise of the vaginal muscles. Ry, you're familiar with several methods for that. Part two, orgasms. Snow, you must have several orgasms per day. Powerful ones, which means you need to practice delayed gratification."

Orgasms—sounded good. Powerful orgasms? *Great.*

"I thought you were a doctor, not a sex therapist," she said, keeping her tone light.

He looked at her, puzzled. "How can the two be separated? Your physical health and sexual health are both part of your essence, connected on every level."

Ryus opened the door. "Need some equipment," he explained. "Back soon."

When the door slid shut, Delos sighed. "That's a relief. I was afraid he wouldn't agree to keep working with you."

She blinked, hurt at the idea that Ryus would reject her. Trying to keep her voice cool, she asked, "Is he your only physical therapist?"

"I have others on staff. But you're good for him. I never thought he'd respond to a Bride. But he certainly responds to you."

A thrilling assessment. Then she recalled how Ryus had left yesterday without a word. "Do you really think so?" she asked wistfully.

The doctor's mouth quirked in a gentle smile. "I gave him a little test today. Now mind you, I'm certain we can rehabilitate you. But I told Ry this morning that I'd made a mistake, bringing you here." With a chuckle, the doctor added, "He was furious—challenged me to a fight. I had to apologize profusely."

Snow glowed, pleased to think Ryus cared that much about her. "Does he challenge people often?"

"Rarely. No one wants to fight him after what happened with Durin—he knows that." He paused expectantly.

She played along. "Tell me what happened."

"Durin used to be notorious for…bothering…other males' wives. There were complaints, but his brother is on the Council, so no one took action."

"Are they very important—the Council members?"

"The Council runs the ship. They hold the power of life and death over all of us."

"So where does Ryus come in?" she asked.

"He challenged Durin. No one else dared to fight a big primus like Durin, with such important connections."

"What happened?"

"The Council declared the battle a draw before they killed each other." The doctor smiled. "But afterward, Durin changed his ways. He doesn't dare face Ry again."

The door beeped and a moment later Ryus entered, carrying a satchel. Snow's gaze lingered on his muscular form. Had he challenged Durin due to disinterested justice? Or had Durin hit on Ryus' wife?

Either way, she admired Ryus' bravery.

Delos rose. "I'm confident you'll do fine," he said, patting her shoulder.

Once the doctor was gone, Ryus gave her the crutches and watched while she attached them. She marveled at how much easier it was today to move and stretch her legs.

"Follow previous pattern," he told her, helping her out of bed. "Walking, then sexual therapy."

Something to look forward to. "I feel stronger today," she said, taking several steps.

"Del expects five percent improvement per day in nerve and muscle tone."

"I guess I've come to the right place." She inhaled deeply, his wonderful scent teasing and arousing her. Much though she was enjoying using her legs, she couldn't wait to lie down and experience his caresses again.

"So tell me about yesterday," she said. "Why did you get upset when I touched you? Are females forbidden to touch males? Tell me the rules."

He gave her a quick, startled glance. "Males enjoy being touched by their females. That was…personal reaction only. Didn't expect to become sexually aroused." He indicated the round, flat disk on the upper portion of his arm. "Anti-erection drug didn't work. Made Del increase the dosage today."

Her allure had overpowered the drug? Good to know.

"Not surprising," he went on. "Most males will think of mating when they look at you."

Now this was a topic she could get into. "Really? What features do Terilian males consider attractive?"

"Rounded hips and buttocks," he answered. "Yours are beautiful. Enticing beyond words. Your black hair is lovely too. Rare with our females. Curls are unknown. Very exotic."

She'd never expected to be a femme fatale. "Since you're on a bigger dose of medication today, maybe you can tell me about the Spring Running? I'm curious."

He hesitated. "People don't talk about it. Religious overtones. Sects have differing beliefs."

"How will I learn if you won't tell me?"

He looked into her face for a long moment. Judging her sincerity? She gazed back at him earnestly.

"All right," he said. "The Spring Running is always held outdoors. Park, jungle, forest. Females enter first, conceal themselves. Sometime later, the quartus and tertius-ranked males are admitted. Hunt for a female and mate. None of those ranks on this ship, though."

"Why not?"

"Only primuses and seconduses were accepted on this venture. Not easy to gain admission. Tests, evaluations, interviews needed to qualify. And high rank."

Snow nodded thoughtfully. So the crème de la crème of their society made up the colonization venture. And a huge number of them — some males, all the wives and children — had been lost to the illness. Such a terrible waste.

"For the upcoming Running, secondus males will be admitted first, then the primuses. A higher-ranked male can take a female away from a lower-ranked male."

Snow thought through all the ramifications of what he'd said. "So a desirable female might mate more than once?"

"Ordinarily couples are faithful. But at the Running…it's an in-between time. Females need to mate constantly until they're satisfied." He added after a moment, "Males too."

Just hearing him talk about it made arousal rush along every nerve.

She thought about mating with two or three different males in the space of an afternoon. While the idea had its exciting aspects, she decided she'd rather wait for Ryus. She couldn't imagine being so fascinated with another male's looks or scent.

After several treks up and down the room, her legs began to tremble. Ryus led her to the bed. "Ready for sexual therapy?"

She nodded eagerly. "Will you get undressed again?"

"If it really matters to you."

"You want me to get aroused, don't you? I like seeing your body."

He didn't answer, but she was able to read his expressions now. Surprisingly, he looked pleased.

While he took his clothes off, she tried to lift her tunic over her head. The struggle made her gasp for breath but she finally succeeded.

He went to the satchel he'd brought and opened it. He brought out the familiar screen-device that measured the strength of her orgasm, laying it on the bedside table.

"Have some things to help you do your vaginal exercises," he said. "Also some other items Terilians enjoy. Feeling adventurous?"

Leather and whips? Her palms grew damp. "Can I refuse if I don't like it?"

"Should know the answer to that already." He showed her the little tube he'd taken out of the satchel. "Start with this. I'll put a little on you, lick it off."

Quivering with anticipation, she lay back against the mattress. He joined her, shaking back his beautiful silver hair. He lay on his side facing her and looked into her eyes. The fiery eagerness in his gaze held her silent.

Opening the tube's cap, he wafted it under her nose. The luscious scent was reminiscent of strawberries.

He squeezed a dollop of it into his palm and rubbed his hands together. Then slowly he moved his palms over her shoulders. The cream heated his fingers to the temperature of a hot bath. She trembled with delight as he smoothed his palms over her shoulder blades, gently tracing bone beneath skin. His hands moved in unison, stroking her collarbone, then downward to caress the sensitive skin framing her breasts.

She held her breath, hoping he would move lower.

He added more cream to his palms, then grasped a breast in each hand. His palms slid against her sensitive flesh, the heat and pressure making her nipples pucker.

Pleasure tendriled down the length of her body, blooming in her pussy. He varied his touch, teasing her by barely brushing his fingertips against each nipple. She lifted her hips, wanting to sob with frustration. She needed more. A harder touch.

Lowering his head, he stroked her right nipple with the tip of his slightly rough tongue. Moisture flooded her pussy.

Sensation danced along her nerves as he licked all around her areola, the strokes of his tongue growing longer, more impassioned. His eyes shut as he moved to her other breast, sucking, licking.

He wanted her. His absorbed expression and his erect cock told her so.

He sucked hard on her left nipple, making her moan with delight. Why didn't he touch her pussy, the way he had yesterday? If she couldn't have his cock then she wanted his fingers stroking her, plunging inside her until she exploded into a powerful climax.

Sensing Snow was close to an orgasm, Ryus drew back.

She whimpered in frustration. "Why did you stop?"

"Del said delayed gratification," he reminded her.

The stormy look in her gray eyes made him think of thunderclouds over the lakelands of Teril. "He isn't here."

That made him smile. "Still have to follow his orders."

"He ordered orgasms," she protested.

He ran his palm over her stomach and down to the curly pelt over her mound, watching as she quivered under his touch. "If you climax too quickly and lightly, your chosen partner won't ejaculate. Trouble is, you're *too* responsive."

She sighed. "I think it's because I went so long without an orgasm after I became too ill to masturbate."

Had he heard correctly? "Your doctor on Earth didn't prescribe sex therapy?"

She looked surprised at the question. "On Earth, doctors rarely think about a patient's sexual health. Until I came aboard this ship, I hadn't had an orgasm for six months."

His pity deepened. Celibacy was difficult enough for males but for a sensual female like Snow, it must have been torture. Now he understood why she craved his caresses. Not because he was special to her. This was pure sexual hunger in a female who'd been starved of life-affirming intimacy.

"Need to exercise your vaginal muscles," he said.

"Will you use your fingers?" she asked eagerly.

"Not this time." Leaning over the side of the bed, he dug through his satchel and found a penile simulator with feedback remote.

Her pink tongue moved over her lips. What if she licked his organ with that quick, sensual motion? Blood rushed downward into his already erect penis, inflaming him further.

He clenched his free hand and released his claws slightly, hoping the pain biting into his palms would counteract his unwanted arousal.

He showed her the simulator. She brightened. "Is that a sex toy?"

"Medical instrument," he said repressively.

"Oh, really? And where could *that* possibly go?" Sarcasm filled her voice. "Let me guess. My armpit?"

He tried to keep his tone objective. "Fits in your vagina. You'll clench your muscles around it." He showed her the feedback remote. "Every time you press hard enough, this light will come on." He stroked her thigh. "Raise your legs and I'll insert it."

Excitement rushed through him. He was going to see her lovely vagina again, the glistening pink lips surrounded by her springy black pelt. The hot, wet tunnel that had contracted so enticingly around his finger the day before.

His engorged penis pushed against his tights. He wanted to mate with her, to feel her clenching around his organ. He glanced down at the simulator with frank envy.

"You'll insert it? That sounds painful." She shifted on the bed and raised her knees. "Maybe you should make sure I'm wet enough to accept it."

The scent of her sweet arousal short-circuited his brain. The simulator was lubricated but he didn't even think of telling her that. Instead he stroked her thighs, ending each caress by brushing his fingers along her labia. Her breathing grew rapid.

"I love it when you touch me," she whispered.

He ached to lavish each part of her lovely body with praise, murmur of the joy he felt when he was with her, tell her how much he cared for her…

No. She's my patient. That's all.

Wet enough? Her cream flowed at his touch. What would she do if he lowered his head and lapped it with his tongue?

Why couldn't he remain professional with this female?

Holding the simulator at the prescribed angle, he gently inserted the head.

"Mmmm, yes!" Her hips rose. "That's *nice*. Push it in deeper."

He inserted it halfway. Her joyful cry stimulated him even more. Would she cry out like that when he filled her with his penis? When he thrust into her while her tight tunnel surrounded his entire length?

"More," she pleaded. The scent of her arousal heightened. Throwing back her head, she moaned.

The rest of it slid in easily. She gasped. "Move it up and down."

"It's for *exercise*," he reminded her. "Make the light come on ten times."

"Then do I get a reward?"

He smiled at the way she bargained. "Agreed."

She nestled her hand into his. The trusting gesture flew straight to his heart. For a moment he was tempted to rub his cheek against hers and mark her with his scent.

But that was a caress between lovers.

She drew a breath. The light on the remote came on. Smiling, he held it up for her to see.

She expelled her breath. "I did it!"

"Well done. Nine more."

Her lovely face determined, she made the light flash five more times. He couldn't help imagining the glorious sensations if he replaced the simulator with his own organ. Would she be shocked if her therapist suggested mating with her? Or would she welcome his attentions?

He desperately needed to get away from her enthralling scent, to walk around the room and regain control.

But he also didn't want to release her hand.

"Four more," he told her.

"The trouble is, that exercise excites me," she confided.

He didn't need to hear that. He could tell by her scent, her flushed face and her swollen labia.

Aroused beyond endurance, he handed her the remote and left the bed. What a cruel trick of nature, that females could masturbate yet males could not. He needed release desperately.

He stalked around the cabin. He'd never had such a difficult assignment.

To hide his discomfort, he went to the satchel again and dug through it.

When he returned to her and stretched out on the bed, she beamed at him. "I did all ten."

"Excellent work." He tried to ignore the way her gaze was drawn to his organ.

How rude she was to stare at Ryus' impressive erection, Snow told herself. But she couldn't help it—it had been so long since she'd seen the glorious sight of a naked man.

He's not a man. He's an alien.

The self-correction did no good. She still wanted to gaze into his gorgeous eyes that sometimes seemed plain brown but often held enticing golden glints. She longed to snuggle against his broad chest and inhale his scent, listen to the rumble of his deep voice, feel his fingers gently parting her damp folds.

He opened his hand, revealing a flat, circular object. "Teaser," he said.

"What does it do?"

Instead of answering, he laid it over her left breast. To her surprise the thin disk that covered her areola was deliciously warm. After a moment it began to move against her breast, exerting a gentle pressure that felt like a sucking mouth.

He watched her, a hint of avidity in his expression. "Like that?"

"Yes!" she gasped. "But I'd rather have *your* mouth."

Startled pleasure lit his face. Lowering his head, he took her right nipple into his mouth.

The wonderful sensations were almost like having two males teasing her sensitive nipples. Excitement flowed directly to her pussy. Involuntarily her muscles clenched around the penile simulator, setting off the light again.

Taking the remote from her, he pressed it. Immediately the simulator began vibrating.

She moaned low in her throat. The delicious breast stimulation plus the deep throbbing within her pussy were incredibly exciting. She thrashed her head from side to side, eager for the climax that was building, building…

The sensations peaked. A racking orgasm surged through her. The pleasure crested and swelled and her pussy pulsed hard around the simulator. Wave after wave rippled through her uncontrollably.

She closed her eyes, enjoying the receding sensations of her climax. Okay, she had to admit he'd been right..."delayed gratification" had been well worth waiting for. And surely today's sensations had been much stronger than yesterday's.

The mattress shifted as he rose.

Disappointed, she tried offering a smile. Why couldn't he stay and cuddle for five lousy minutes?

Forgetting he was her physical therapist and not her lover put her heart at risk. The thought made her bite her lip. Who was she kidding? Her heart was already at risk.

He yanked his tunic over his head. Then quickly picking up the screen-device, he frowned at it.

"Will you tell me this time or make me worry until Dr. Delos arrives tomorrow?"

"Doing better. But still not strong enough."

She couldn't stop thinking about his beautiful, erect cock. "I'd have a better climax if we actually mated," she said, surprising herself with the bold statement. "Don't get me wrong, the touching's very nice—but it's just not the same as real intercourse."

His dark eyebrows drew down. "Unprofessional."

"*Now* you're worried about professional behavior? When you've aided and abetted a mass kidnapping?"

He snatched up his tights. With a final glare, he left the room.

*****

Stalking into Delos' office, Ryus found the doctor dictating to Belmarra. After one look at him, Delos broke off in mid-sentence.

"Give Snow another therapist," Ryus demanded, banging down the screen-device on Del's desk. "Can't maintain my objectivity."

Instead of responding to these entirely valid concerns, Delos picked up the device. "Impressive gain since yesterday," he observed. "You must be doing something right."

"That's not the point."

"Did you walk her around the room? How did she do?"

"Fine." Ryus didn't even try to restrain his growl. *That's not the point.*

"Oh, I think it is." Delos gave him his usual imperturbable smile. "We're here for the good of our patients. No one knows better than me how hard it is to work with these beautiful Earthian females. I'm confident you'll manage."

Why was Del being so obtuse? Maybe he needed a little intimidation. Ryus leaned over the desk, releasing his claws. "Now listen to me—" he growled.

Delos folded his arms. Instead of backing away, as Ryus expected, he leaned in closer. "*You* listen to *me*. And you can put your claws away because I won't fight you no matter what insult you dream up. Snow needs to gain enough strength to be a Bride. That's all I care about—her welfare. Stop whining and *do your job*."

Ryus stared at him, astonished the doctor dared to speak this way to a male who outranked him.

"She asked me to *mate* with her." He waited for Del to reel back in shock.

"Great idea—go right ahead." Delos turned to his computer screen. "Is that all? I'm extremely busy."

"Are you serious?" Ryus demanded.

"Someone has to be the first." Delos tapped his computer screen. If he was pretending to be absorbed in work, he was doing an excellent job of it. "Better for her to mate with you than to be thrown unprepared into the Spring Running. Even if it's weeks away, she'll still be weaker than the other females."

"Can't believe you're condoning this!"

Delos turned and scrutinized his expression. In a somewhat kinder voice, he added, "Nothing about this situation is normal. I trust your judgment."

"Don't. All I can think about is her beauty, her voice, her scent…" He sounded like a lovesick fool. Why wouldn't Del listen?

"Do your best. Report back after you've mated with her." Delos returned to the computer screen, ignoring Ryus' menacing growl.

* * * * *

Snow wiped the sweat off her brow and kept moving. The electronic crutches gave her the confidence she needed to navigate the room unescorted. Maybe Ryus wouldn't approve that she was exercising without him, but who cared what he thought?

An entire day had passed without his presence. What could he possibly be doing? Wasn't he supposed to be there every day, providing therapy?

A male who considered it "unprofessional" to make love to her didn't deserve to have his opinion taken into account. She'd show him. She'd get stronger every day. At the Spring Running, she'd mate with the handsomest male she could find. Maybe more than one. Ryus would curse himself, realizing how he'd missed out…

The door slid open. Snow flinched and nearly fell. The gravity field around the crutches steadied her.

Ryus strode into the room. His brows drew together in disapproval.

"Don't you believe in knocking?" she demanded.

"Belmarra told me what you were doing. Shouldn't exercise by yourself."

"Who's Belmarra and why is she spying on me?"

"Ship's computer. Watches all patients. Five doctors, one thousand patients — it's necessary."

"Then she can let you know if I need you. Right now, I don't." Turning her back on him, she slowly made her way toward the bed.

Uncomfortable beneath his intent gaze, she sat heavily on the bed. She suppressed a gasp for breath, not wanting to reveal her exhaustion.

He came closer, putting his hands on her shoulders. The heat of his palms penetrated down to her bones, making her feel soothed and protected. She wanted him in bed with her, pleasuring her with those clever, gentle fingers.

Judging by his fiery expression, he wanted the same thing.

Would he lick her breasts again, tease her nipples until they peaked? A pulse beat between her legs. She pressed her thighs together, trying not to breathe in his compelling scent.

She mustn't forget she was angry with him. "I told you to leave."

His growl rumbled through the room. "Bold speech, from a female to a primus." He released her shoulders.

Laughter surged from her throat. "If you expect deference from the women you've kidnapped, you're going to be disappointed."

Instead of looking angry, as she'd expected, Ryus' expression grew thoughtful. "Many adjustments ahead. More than the Council foresees."

Snow nodded. Were the Terilians really prepared to deal with a thousand pissed off Earthians? "Where are the women now?" she asked. "Are they all in cabins like mine?" Suddenly she longed to see a human face.

"Not yet." He held out his hands. "Come. We'll go to them."

Chapter Four

Like hundreds of Sleeping Beauties, the women lay unconscious in narrow hospital beds. Clinging to Ryus' arm, Snow walked down row after row, peering into their serene faces. They were well tended—sweet-smelling, hair combed, colorful tunics fresh.

While all races from Earth were represented, the women had one thing in common. None of them was slender. Everywhere she looked, Snow saw voluptuous breasts and rounded hips.

"Selfish of us," Ryus commented. "From millions of eligible Earth females, we chose the most intelligent and beautiful. Earth's loss is our gain."

His words made her glow inside. Okay, she'd always known she was intelligent. She'd earned her doctorate in history before the age of twenty-eight. But no one had ever considered her beautiful. Until now.

Interspersed throughout the room, Terilian males walked among the women, adjusting feeding tubes, rubbing lotions, providing sponge baths.

"Are they all doctors?" Snow asked.

"When the Brides first arrived, a call went out for Sick Bay orderlies. Almost every male on board volunteered." Ryus' tone took on a note of amusement. "Even the primuses, who aren't used to manual labor."

"They all wanted to be near the Brides?"

"Every one of us was starving for the sight and scent of females."

A wave of sympathy rippled through her. How desolate it must have been for the survivors of the great illness, mourning their wives and young. Would the women around her understand the Terilians' plight? Would they forgive the crime?

Snow became aware of covert scrutiny from the nearest orderlies. One was a big male, somewhat older than Ryus, with golden hair and intent blue eyes. The other was slender, his long black hair caught up in a complex arrangement of braids and copper jewelry. They were both ridiculously handsome—or maybe she thought so because she was growing accustomed to the Terilian appearance. Their stiff mustaches, small noses and furry cat ears were inhuman, but attractive in their own way.

The slender male smiled at her. Flattered by the attention, Snow smiled back.

Ryus' growl made her flinch. "Get on with your work," he commanded the orderly, who quickly lowered his eyes and turned to his patient.

The golden-haired male was not so easily intimidated. Coming closer, he said, "Ry, introduce me to your charming companion." His gaze lingered on Snow's face.

"Snow Jarrett, behold Primus Hirdos of the Golden Pelt, Council member." Ryus' voice was deeply reluctant, as though he regretted making the introduction.

The Council runs the ship, Delos had told her. *They hold the power of life and death over all of us.* Worried, she looked up into Hirdos' eyes.

He smiled reassuringly. "Tell me, Snow Jarrett, is everyone treating you well?"

Ryus has provided several wonderful orgasms. Repressing a giggle, she answered demurely, "They've all been kind."

"Come, Snow—must keep walking," Ryus said, turning abruptly and propelling her away from Hirdos.

"Why did that black-haired male listen to you?" Snow asked as Ryus hurried her down the next row of women, away from the two orderlies. "Do you outrank him?"

"He's a primus like me—males don't wear jewelry unless they're primus-ranked. He could either back down or fight me. Chose not to fight."

She remembered Delos' story about the altercation between Ryus and Durin. It was hard to imagine Ryus in a battle, since he'd always been so gentle with her.

"Do males and females ever fight each other?" she asked.

Ryus' quick glance at her revealed his shock. "A male would never risk harming a female. The other males would kill him."

Thinking of a friend who'd been stalked and beaten by an ex-lover, Snow was glad to hear about Terilian justice.

"Sometimes mates mock-wrestle without claws," Ryus added. "Foreplay."

She pictured squirming away from his hands, being caught and licked while she struggled. He'd yank down his tights, then pin her arms above her head and thrust into her. Heat flashed through her pussy.

Without a word being said, somehow he sensed the lust surging through her. "Arousing?" he asked, dropping his voice. "Maybe when you're stronger, little one."

The steel-muscled arm under her hand trembled. Her excitement was affecting him. Thrilled at the thought, she longed to return to her cabin with him. Wasn't it time for more sexual therapy? Hadn't the doctor ordered "powerful orgasms"?

Ryus' hand hovered uncertainly by the drug disk on his arm. "Must speak to Del." He gestured toward the doctor, who was examining a woman across the room. "Back soon."

After he'd gone, Snow continued her slow walk among her fellow Earthians, compelled to examine their faces. The odds were millions to one that she'd find any of her single or divorced friends, but she kept searching.

What would the others think when they awoke? Would they mourn the relatives and friends left behind? Or would they bond together on the voyage, looking forward to conquering the new planet?

Which ones would become her friends?

"Small female!" The male who confronted her was larger even than Ryus. His rust-colored hair streamed to his waist. Leaning forward, he stared into her eyes. "How delicious your alien flesh smells. But why are you the only one awake?" He put his hand on her shoulder, fingering her silky tunic.

His touch was an invasion. Instinctively she jerked back. Her knees buckled with the sudden movement but the gravity field caught her before she fell.

The huge male looked down at her legs, scowling. "Why are you using crutches?" he demanded. "Are you sickly?"

Why should she fear him? She forced herself to stand her ground, even though his fierce questions were obviously meant to be intimidating.

"I *was* sick," she admitted. "Dr. Delos cured me."

"If you're cured, why are the crutches necessary? I argued against ill females being brought onto the ship." His contemptuous gaze swept over her. "A sickly weakling can't satisfy a Terilian male!" He took a step toward her, backing her against one of the beds. "What use are you?"

She looked around for Ryus. Unfortunately he was many yards away, speaking to the doctor, his back to her. She'd have to fight this battle herself.

Assuming the stern expression she'd used when a student became unruly, she said, "Where I come from, males are polite to women who are strangers. You should learn some manners from Earth."

The huge male's eyes opened wide with outrage. Snow braced herself for another rude remark.

Dr. Delos gestured at them. Ryus whirled around. In seconds he came bounding across the room. His speed astonished her. When he launched himself into the air and sailed over five rows of Brides, she gasped. So much raw power in that effortless leap, twice the height and distance of a human pole-vaulter.

Landing lightly on his feet behind her, Ryus laid his hands on her shoulders, his touch light but comforting. "What are you doing in Sick Bay, Durin?" he demanded.

Durin...so this was the one who had bothered other male's wives. The one who had fought Ryus.

Ignoring Ryus' question, Durin asked, "Why is this female awake while the others sleep?"

"Not your business," Ryus growled.

"The Brides are everyone's business." Durin gazed at Ryus' hands. "Is this one special to you?"

"She's my patient." Ryus' fingers tightened protectively against her skin.

"No wonder you have her concealed. Her feebleness is disgusting."

Snow winced at the insult. Was that how most of the Terilians would see her? A disgusting invalid who never should have been brought aboard? Her fingernails dug into her palms.

Hurrying closer, Dr. Delos was just in time to hear the comment. "There's no concealment. The Council is aware of this Bride's *temporary* infirmity." His tone was sharper than she'd ever heard it. "No one is admitted to Sick Bay except for orderlies and therapists. Durin, I must ask you to leave."

Bending forward until he was nose to nose with the doctor, Durin said, "And I must ask *you* to remember my rank when you address me, Secondus Delos."

Unmoving, the doctor glared at him. "I tended your wounds after your battle with Ryus. Don't make me regret saving your life."

Durin growled, unsheathing a set of terrifying, copper-hued claws. Even one of them looked like it could slice through steel—and there were ten on display.

Ryus released Snow and stepped forward to face Durin. "Another fight?" Ryus asked.

"No!" Snow and Delos spoke simultaneously. The doctor grasped Ryus' arm. "Therapist Ryus, your duty is to your patient."

Ryus ignored him, as did Durin. Tension throbbed through the room. Snow held her breath. Was an attack imminent?

Durin took a step back. "We'll see what my brother has to say."

She remembered that Durin's brother was a Council member. Damp with sudden perspiration, she wondered if she'd become a bone of contention between Durin and Ryus.

"Dung-picker," Ryus said as the door slid shut behind Durin. "Should have killed him when I had the chance."

His face stern, Delos tapped his shoulder in agreement.

Snow's knees trembled. Before she realized what he was going to do, Ryus swooped her into his arms, cradling her against his broad chest. The humming fear racing along her nerves dissipated. Closing her eyes, she relaxed and inhaled his minty scent.

"Take Snow back to her room," the doctor said. "And follow through on what we discussed earlier."

*****

Seething with rage, Ryus strode down the corridor, Snow nestled in his arms. His hatred of Durin, already strong, had intensified tenfold. He'd been tempted to match claws again with the other male, without the necessary formal challenge.

Her feebleness is disgusting. How dared Durin use such a word when speaking of Snow? A slash across the mouth would make him withdraw that insult...

Grimacing, Ryus came to an unexpected conclusion. He was brave enough to fight Durin but not brave enough to mate with Snow.

If there was one thing he despised, it was cowardice. He'd come to Snow's cabin an hour ago fully intending to mate with her. Yet instead of speaking the sweet words that came to mind in her company, he'd picked a fight with her. Then he'd taken her to Sick Bay so that he wouldn't have to lie down next to her, fondle her enticing breasts and mate with her.

What did he fear? His wife would never return. He'd known that for two years.

He recalled the horrifying thrill he'd experienced when Snow fondled him. If he were honest with himself, he'd admit to wanting that again.

Involuntarily, his arms tightened around her. Making a tiny noise of pleasure, she laid her palm against his chest, stroking his skin. Waves of delight crashed through him.

"Where are we going?" she asked. "Wasn't that my cabin we just passed? Or am I confused?"

"Going to my cabin. Thought you might like to see it."

"Oh! Yes, I would." The sweet curve of her lips and her eager eyes filled him with longing. He had to stop then, unable to resist nibbling the smooth length of her neck. She moaned and gripped his shoulders. Her scent pleaded with him to mate with her.

He had to keep walking. He forced himself to draw back, shaking his head in an attempt to clear it.

Blinking, he realized he was at the silver-etched door of his cabin. He jammed his palm against the scanner. The door opened. A few strides and a leap brought them to the high bed.

Snow gasped, her fingers digging into his shoulders. "You could have warned me!"

"Sorry. Easy to forget you don't know everything about us. Especially when you're so much like a Terilian female."

"I am?" Releasing him, she settled herself against the slightly elevated back of the bed. "Durin said I was disgusting."

He moved closer, stroking her black curls to reassure her. "Take no heed of him. Insult was directed at me, not you."

Her gaze held his. "Are you sure? I know you and the doctor are nice—but maybe the other Terilian males will reject me."

"Won't reject you." The idea of another male taking her was like the torture of a nerve-agonizer across his pelt. She was his. His alone. "They'll want to mate with you."

"Like you do?" Her eyes still meeting his, she gave a sinuous wiggle.

No longer able to resist her, he jerked down the top of her tunic. Her nipples were flushed and peaking, asking to be sucked. He feasted his eyes on them, drinking in their beauty.

She grabbed his hand and steered it to her breast. "Please, Ryus."

He lowered his head to her right breast, teasing it with his tongue while he rolled her left nipple between his fingers. Her breathing shortened as he worked both nipples. He bit down lightly, letting her feel his teeth against the hardened flesh. She cried out, her back arching.

"I want you so much," she whispered, parting her legs. The scent of her heightened arousal nearly drove him mad. His groin tightened, his organ lengthening, pushing against his tights, seeking out the pleasure only she could provide.

Who would have thought these Earth women would be so responsive to Terilian males? *She wants me. She wants me to mate with her.* Sweet balm for his long solitude. Two years alone…how had he endured?

First he had to ensure she was at the peak of arousal. Moving downward on the bed, he teased her navel with his tongue while he gently stroked the damp curls back from her clitoris. Her hips moved restlessly.

This close to the seat of her pleasure, her scent overwhelmed him. He ached to thrust into her, to fill her channel with his hard organ until she shrieked with excitement. He struggled to retain control, knowing the primary goal was her delight, not his own satisfaction.

Lowering his head, he licked slowly up her outer lips, thrilled when she trembled and cried out.

"Ryus!" He loved it when she spoke his name. "So good…" she sighed. "I never thought I'd have this again."

Neither had he.

He licked again, taking his time, noting the way her breathing quickened and her scent intensified.

Snow couldn't help it. She had to cry aloud, a jagged keening that was almost a sob, when Ryus' tongue penetrated her damp folds. He licked all around the entrance to her vagina, sometimes teasing lightly, sometimes swirling his tongue upward, flicking against her clit.

She couldn't hold her hips still. She lifted them, wordlessly asking for more. God, how she wanted more. And yet she wanted to remain like this, enjoying the incredible movements of his warm tongue while dangling on the edge of pleasure.

He raised his head. "Like it?"

He had to be teasing. He must know how thrilled she was by his skillful attentions to her pussy. Couldn't he tell by her moans and cries? By the way she was quivering? By her wanton thrusting against his mouth?

"I need more. Please!" she begged shamelessly.

"Ready to mate?" He moved upward on the bed, straddling her. His cock was engorged, ready to plunge inside her eager pussy.

She'd known him only a few days but it seemed like she'd been waiting forever to make love with him. Raising her hips, she whispered, "I want you inside me."

A soft chime filled the cabin. A feminine voice spoke. "Your pardon, Primus Ryus. The Council summons you and Earth female Snow Jarrett. Report to Level Four Council Chamber immediately."

Ryus froze. "Tell them five minutes, Belmarra."

Tempted to burst into tears of frustration and anger, she said, "Why didn't you say thirty minutes? We could have finished!"

He looked shocked. "A summons from the Council can't be ignored." His forehead creasing, he lifted her hand to his cheek. "We'll return to this later. Promise."

Mollified by the tender gesture, she cleaned herself with the towel he gave her. Once dressed, they took the elevator to Level Four.

Snow was glad of Ryus' powerful form beside her as they entered the Council Chamber. The Council members knelt on stools, lined up on one side of a long table. Durin stood to the left. She also recognized Hirdos, whom she'd met in Sick Bay.

The six males gazed at her, examining every inch of her from her shoes to the curls on top of her head. For a moment she wanted to quail away from their unabashed scrutiny.

The Terilians needed her and her fellow Earth women. They would die without mating. The thought made her lift her chin proudly and meet the Council's bold stares without fear.

The black-haired male closest to Durin retained his stern expression. He looked familiar—when had she seen him before? But the flickering smiles on other males' faces heartened her. Hirdos licked his lips.

She was the first female they'd been near in two years—or at least, the only one who was conscious.

Ryus took a step forward. "Why this summons?" he asked, his deep voice harsh and abrupt. "Interrupted a crucial therapy session."

Therapy! He'd been about to make love to her. Hadn't their relationship moved beyond therapist-patient?

The black-haired male said, "We're awaiting one more person, Ryus. Kindly restrain your impatience." His voice pricked her memory. He was the male who had appeared on Earth television to announce the mass kidnapping. *Primus Taddus of the Black-Striped Pelt.*

The door slid open, admitting Dr. Delos. With a swift look around, he assessed the situation then addressed the Council. "Good primuses, I hope this session will be short. I've just awakened the first fifty Brides. As you can imagine, my orderlies and I are extremely pressed for time."

Snow quivered with anticipation, thrilled to hear that other women were conscious. She turned toward Delos, about to bombard him with questions. But the Council members were already interrogating him. "Are the Earth females angry? Confused? Do they remember why they're here? When can we see them? How soon can we hold the Spring Running?"

Taddus and Durin exchanged frustrated looks. Snow realized what the doctor had done—successfully diverted the Council's attention from her to their future Brides.

With a crash of his fist on the table, Taddus brought silence to the room. "Let us not ignore our current business. Durin came to us, concerned by the weakness of Snow Jarrett, who stands before us today wearing crutches. Secondus Delos' own medical reports suggest that she is not yet strong enough to fulfill her duties as a Bride. Doctor, what can you add to this discussion?"

Delos took a step forward. "Snow's strength increases daily. Given time, she will be as strong as any other Earth female."

"But time is what we lack," Durin said. "Delos, wasn't it you who proved to the Council that we would die unless we mated? Our task now is to ensure the females are ready for the Spring Running. We can't let our purpose be diverted by this sickly one—*who never should have been brought aboard*!"

A chill ran down Snow's spine when one of the Council members touched his shoulder, indicating agreement with Durin.

Then Hirdos spoke. "You're too hasty, Durin. We all agreed that a percentage of the Earth females could have illnesses. Many of us believe that stealing the females was wrong but necessary. Curing them—giving them a better life—mitigates our guilt."

"*Curing* them, Hirdos," Durin exclaimed. "But Snow Jarrett is still sick!"

Ryus' menacing growl echoed through the room, which fell silent. "Snow *is* cured," he said. "Her weakness is a matter for therapy. She's getting it." He surveyed the Council, frowning. "Talking just wastes time."

"It's not so simple," Durin said. "I contend Snow Jarrett cannot be a Bride."

A Council member whose gray hair was striped with brown spoke up, his tone worried. "Impossible! If this female does not become a Bride, one of our males will be left unwed."

To Snow's horror, Durin gestured at Ryus. "*He* declared himself morally opposed to the theft of Earth females. Let him prove his sincerity by forgoing the Spring Running." His glance slid to Snow. "Since she is no use to us, she should disembark at Jahariz, the last stop before we reach our new home. That is the humane solution."

"That dismal swamp of a planet?" Ryus demanded. Fury seemed to roll off him in waves. "I'll challenge every one of you before I let that happen."

His support gave her a warm tingle of pleasure. Still, this had gone on long enough.

"I can't believe this discussion." Snow strode forward until she was mere inches from the Council's table. About to launch into a furiously indignant speech, she paused.

Her increased proximity was having an unmistakable effect on the Council members. Their entranced gazes were fixed on her body. Their nostrils flared as they drank in her scent. Hirdos, in a motion that seemed involuntary, reached his hand toward her.

Despite the tension in the room, a thrill coursed along her veins. On Earth, she'd been too ordinary to manipulate men through her feminine allure. Here she was beautiful. And this crisis was important enough to require the use of her new power.

"Good primuses," she said, imitating the way Dr. Delos had addressed them, "please don't reject me so unkindly. I'm happy to be here among you, growing healthier and stronger every day. Grant me the time to regain my full strength." She lowered her voice to a sensual purr. "I'm very eager to be a Bride." She reached her hand up, caressing her neck in a slow, seductive movement. If she'd stripped her clothes off and revealed her naked body, she couldn't have riveted their attention more thoroughly.

"I yearn for a husband's caress." *For Ryus' caress.* Her fingers moved through her hair, fluffing it, releasing its scent.

Durin was her enemy. Yet even he leaned forward, his chest rising and falling quickly.

Hirdos frowned at him. "How dare you propose sending this enticing female into exile? Are you heartless?"

Another male chimed in, "We should trust Delos' prognosis."

Two of them were on her side, thank goodness. She smiled warmly at the male who'd just spoken, gratified when he smiled back, gazing into her eyes.

"It is unseemly for the female to be present while we decide her fate," Taddus said. "You two—" A wave of his hand indicated Ryus and Delos. "Take her into the adjoining chamber."

"Durin is excused as well," Hirdos said. "He is not a Council member."

Taddus glared at him but Hirdos looked back impassively. Finally Taddus touched his shoulder in agreement.

Ryus took Snow's arm, leading her from the room. Delos and Durin followed.

The adjoining chamber was empty, except for six stools and a huge wall screen showing three-dimensional scenes of leafy vegetation waving in the breeze. Ryus took her to a stool then moved away, pacing restlessly around the room. Durin stood by the door, his gaze fixed on Ryus.

Snow's hands, flat on her thighs, curled into fists. How unfair, to kidnap her from Earth and then dump her on a swamp-planet. She'd have been better off dying in the nursing home.

The doctor drew up a stool beside her. Gesturing at the picture, he said in his kindly way, "The holograph shows Gazeem, our new planet."

He was trying to distract her during this anxious waiting. She knew that but turned obediently toward the screen.

A dense forest of ancient trees. Turquoise leaves rippled as though teased by the wind. Patches of sky shone rosy pink, glimmering through the thick white clouds. Then beams of sun broke through and thousands of branches lifted simultaneously, a chorus praising the light.

Snow drew a delighted breath. "*That's* where we're headed? It's so beautiful." Then remembering why they were waiting, she added, "I hope I get there."

Coming up behind her, Ryus said, "You will." He put his hands on her shoulders. She sighed, relaxing under his warm, reassuring touch. "Don't doubt it, little one."

"Surely that's for the Council to decide," Durin said.

Ryus turned to look at Durin, eyes narrowing. If only he hadn't betrayed to Durin how much he cared for Snow. He'd handed his enemy a control-pad for vengeance.

He should have been more cautious.

A futile thought. He remembered one of the proverbs of his Peltdom. "Love, like rotting meat, can never be concealed."

Not that he *loved* Snow. He couldn't let a woman of Earth hold the same place in his heart that Arooa had held.

Yet somehow Snow had found her own place.

As they waited, Snow plied Del with questions about the awakened brides. Ryus barely listened, more interested in watching Snow's varied expressions as the doctor spoke. Was she more enticing when she frowned thoughtfully, her face revealing her keen intelligence? Or when she flashed her lovely smile?

One thing he knew for certain. As long as he was alive, Snow would never be ousted from the ship.

At last they were called back into the meeting room. Ryus scanned the Council members. Had they had come to a wise decision? Or would he have to challenge all of them? With difficulty, he kept his claws sheathed. Asher, somewhat undersized, would not want to fight. Hirdos had already shown himself to be Snow's ally. But what of Taddus? Back on Teril, he had challenged and killed a member of the Brown-striped Pelt who had insulted his illustrious father. Taddus would be a worthy opponent.

Scenting Snow's apprehension, Ryus put his arm around her waist. A quiver ran through her body. Yet her expression was fearless as she looked each Council member in the eye. The lone human in the room, she faced those who would decide her fate without flinching. Couldn't the Council see that Snow was the type of female needed to forge a new life on Gazeem? What did physical strength matter compared to her shining courage?

Taddus looked at Ryus, his expression severe. "Primus Ryus of the Silver Pelt, you claim that Snow Jarrett is fit to be a Bride. You have even dared to challenge this Council. However, we have decided that dueling is not the way to solve this complex problem.

"Instead, we have settled on a procedure that will allow us to determine whether Snow may participate in the upcoming Spring Running. Ryus and Snow…today, while the Council observes you, you must mate."

Chapter Five

In the room adjoining the Council Chamber, Snow glared at Ryus and Delos. The Terilian males wore identical puzzled expressions.

"How dare the Council suggest such a thing!" Snow exclaimed. "They're nothing but voyeurs!"

"Don't understand your objection," Ryus said. "Haven't you ever mated with others present?"

"Of course not!" Snow declared. "I'm being treated like a—" She groped for a word and found no Terilian equivalent for "prostitute". Was it possible that sex workers didn't exist in this culture? "Like a woman who is selling the use of her vagina for money."

Ryus' nostrils flared as though he smelled something disgusting. "Are there really such people on Earth?"

Delos sounded equally sickened as he said, "Indeed, the sale of sexual acts is considered a viable profession there. Snow, please do not speak of it again."

"So you find it shocking?" she asked. "I'm just as shocked by the idea of mating in public."

"Why?" Ryus said. "Many people find it amusing to mate while others watch. The ship has rooms on the Third Level for that very purpose." His voice rose in enthusiasm. "Some couples practice for days, perfecting a particularly engrossing technique, before they exhibit it to their friends." With a sigh, he added, "Talking about the past, of course."

Snow fell silent. When she'd first heard the Council's decision, she'd imagined they were treating her, an Earth woman, with disrespect. Surely they wanted to watch merely for the titillation value.

But maybe she had it all wrong. If this was a normal part of their culture, she was not being treated like a prostitute. Maybe the Council really wanted to judge her interaction with Ryus.

Delos' serious voice cut through her musing. "No one can force you to do this, Snow. But believe me, it'll be preferable to having Ryus duel every Council member. Strong as he is, he could be badly wounded, even killed."

Ryus threw an impatient look at the doctor. "Give us a moment alone, Del."

Delos rose immediately. "I'm going to Sick Bay. The Council can let me know if they need me."

As soon as the door shut behind him, Ryus came to her, taking her in his arms. "Don't listen to Del. Underestimates me."

Snow relaxed against him, breathing in his scent, comforted by the feel of his broad chest, his strong arms holding her. "I don't want you to fight. Maybe it would be better to do what they want."

He drew back, tilting her chin up with gentle fingers so he could look into her eyes. "Since the day we met, I've wanted to mate with you. Never thought I'd feel that way again. With you, it's *all* I think about." He cradled the side of her face in his warm palm. She trembled under his caressing touch. Surely he cared for her. Surely this was love, not therapy.

"I'm not certain…" She hated being indecisive. She wanted to have sex with Ryus. She'd wanted him from the instant she'd opened her eyes and looked at him, the day she awoke. When he held her like this, her nipples tightened and her pussy tingled.

But could she really mate with him while the entire Council watched?

Ryus' hands moved slowly down her back, ending with his palms on her buttocks. His strong hands massaged the plump mounds through her thin tunic. Instantly heat rushed through her pussy. She moaned, longing for more.

"Don't do this out of fear or to keep me from dueling." His voice went low. "But if you want me as much as I want you — if your body aches to mate with me — if you want to feel my hands and tongue and penis giving you pleasure — then consider doing what they ask."

She'd rarely heard so many words from him at once. The conviction and caring in his voice pleased her more than if he'd written an ode in her honor.

Looking up into his eyes, the color of warm, dark honey, she saw a spark that took her breath away. She remembered how she'd felt on her first and last day in the nursing home. *Christmas in July*. She'd been frozen to her chilly white bed, barely able to move, sure she'd never be warm again.

Now the ice had thawed. Even better, she blazed with desire, a flame that would consume her if left unsatisfied.

"Little one…" His hands molded her buttocks, pressing her against him so that she felt the hot length of his hard cock. "Will you mate with me in front of the Council?"

She whispered, "Yes."

* * * * *

Snow lay against the elevated back of the round bed that had been brought into the meeting room, trying to calm herself with deep breaths. She still wore her pink tunic. Somehow appearing unclothed in front of the Council seemed more nerve-racking than mating in front of them.

Clearly Ryus suffered no such inhibitions. He yanked his gray tunic over his head, then loosened his silver hair from the band that held it back. With a shake of his powerful shoulders, his long hair spilled out over his naked chest.

Her gaze traveled from the rippling muscles of his torso to his corded neck and finally to his handsome face. His eyes studied her while his chest rose and fell rapidly. He wanted her more than any male had ever desired her before.

His desperate arousal heightened her own excitement.

Five males watched silently. "The mating test is for the Council alone," Hirdos had declared, calling for a vote. Only Taddus had voted for Durin to remain. And so Durin, in spite of his protests, had been ordered to vacate the room. Snow felt slightly more comfortable without his malign presence.

As Ryus came toward the bed, she reached her arms out, welcoming him.

Smiling at her eagerness, he tugged his tights down and stepped out of them. His swollen cock was thick and dark against his stomach. Her mouth went dry as she stared at it. It had been years since she'd felt a man's cock inside her, thrilling her with its delightful invasion.

Her pussy throbbed. Why didn't he hurry to the bed? She wanted his hands stroking her breasts, his hot mouth sliding over her skin. And most of all, she wanted his cock thrusting inside her pussy.

She already knew the incredible sensations his hands and mouth brought her. But now she hungered for more. She'd lain quietly under his caresses long enough. The next step was to share the joy with him, to show him the pleasure he'd receive in her bed.

One of the Council members whispered to another, "The Earth female is eager to mate with Ryus." Perhaps his words weren't meant for her, but her enhanced hearing revealed them.

The sudden distraction overwhelmed her. What was she thinking, to allow herself to be so wanton? What was she doing here, about to have sex with an alien while other aliens watched? Her thudding heart skipped a beat.

Ryus joined her on the bed, kneeling between her legs. Gazing into her eyes, he put his hands on her shoulders. His palms moved slowly down her arms.

"You're trembling," he said. The concern in his voice soothed her. "Remember what I told you, our first day together."

No one will hurt you.

Her heart pounded still, but now it was from anticipation. "I'm all right," she whispered. "Let's give them their show."

"This isn't for them." The corners of his mouth lifted. "This is for you and me." He leaned forward. Would he kiss her at last? Instead he rubbed his cheek against hers. The sweet intimacy of the gesture touched her. In return, she whispered his name.

His wonderful minty scent intensified, intoxicating her, mesmerizing her. The other males in the room seemed to fade away.

His palms closed around her breasts, letting her feel the powerful warmth of his hands through the sheer fabric. He massaged and pressed, forcing a moan from her. Her pussy responded with a flood of moisture.

His fingers moved to the metal clasps at the neckline of her tunic. He gave her a questioning look. She murmured, "Go ahead." Why had she left her tunic on, an annoying layer between her skin and his hands?

He flipped the clasps. Her tunic fell open, the silky fabric slithering downward. A collective sigh went up from the males in the room as her breasts were revealed, her nipples swollen and peaking from Ryus' touch.

"By the Great Fur-Mother," Hirdos whispered. "Snow Jarrett brings us a rich dowry of beauty." He was answered with murmurs of agreement.

So they thought she was beautiful? A mad impulse to display herself to them overtook her. She cupped her breasts in her hands, squeezing them together and lifting them toward

Ryus. With a startled sound, somewhere between a growl and a groan, he bent swiftly, taking her left breast in his mouth. His roughened tongue laved the nipple again and again. Hot waves of pleasure shot down her body, pooling in her pussy.

Her breath came short and fast. He switched to her other breast, sucking until her nipple was flushed and hard.

From far away, Hirdos' voice came to her ears. "I'd give my entire fortune to be in Ry's place."

She told the bed to lower the back. Ryus stretched out beside her, on her right, his mouth still teasing her breasts while his hand roved over her thighs. She turned her head to the left. The Council members sat behind their table. Their eyes were bright, fixed on her without blinking. Hirdos leaned forward, his pale skin flushed. Taddus, his hand under his tunic, was stroking his cock.

They all envied Ryus. They all wanted to be in bed with her, about to mate with her. Their lustful glances added to her arousal.

How long had it been since a man had made love to her? And now here she was with Ryus, the Terilian she'd hungered for since her first sight of him.

Her hand closed around his thick shaft. He gasped when she slid her palm up its burning-hot length. She gloried in the softness of his skin and the steel-hard core underneath it.

He raised up on his elbows, chest shuddering. "Stop," he whispered, his tone desperate, "or we'll have to mate immediately."

In her entire life, she'd never heard more welcome words. "Yes, that's what I want."

His golden gaze brimmed with a mixture of lust and concern. "Sure?" he asked, even as he moved into position between her legs. His hair fell around them like a shining curtain, sealing them into their own world of silver.

She sensed the rabid eagerness humming through him, an eagerness that matched her own. His body was demanding that he plunge into her but he held back, wanting to make sure she was ready. How she admired the control he was keeping over himself—for her sake.

Someone on the Council said, "Watching this is torture." Difficult indeed, to watch without release. Of the males in the room, only Ryus would be lucky enough to climax...if her own orgasm was strong enough. She prayed it would be.

She parted her thighs, drawing her knees up. "I want you so much," she told him, longing plain in her voice. "*Now.*"

Her swollen, naked pussy was exposed to every male in the room. She heard the collective gasp from the Council and Ryus' excited growl.

Nothing mattered except her urgent need for him.

"I'd like to lap the cream from those pretty lips," Hirdos said.

"If this one were mine, I'd give her orgasm after orgasm," Taddus declared. "We must hold the Running soon."

Holding his cock by the base, Ryus rubbed it up and down her slit. The teasing movement made her even wetter, easing his cock's entrance as it pushed against her opening. For just a moment, his heat and size frightened her. It had been so long... She panted as he pressed forward, his thick cock head stretching her.

He paused, giving her a chance to relish the thrills racing through her.

"Don't stop," she pleaded, digging her nails into his back.

He advanced a few inches then paused again. "All right?"

She responded by lifting her hips, taking more of his long shaft inside her. After a moment her tightness gave way.

And the pleasure began.

With a groan he plunged in deep, filling her with his hard length. She cried out, almost unable to bear the intense sensations.

He pulled back. Somehow that was even better. A sound of primitive satisfaction spilled from her throat. She wanted to tell him, "More—more!" but already he was thrusting into her again.

She began moving with him. Unbelievably her passion mounted. She choked out his name.

His mouth trembled. "Snow." Her name was so simple but he sounded as though he could barely force the word from his lips. His chest heaved. "My beautiful Snow." Lowering his head, he sucked her nipple into his hot mouth.

The Council watched, their faces revealing arousal and lust. Several were fondling their cocks…but only Ryus would mate today, she thought. Only Ryus would climax.

His lips pulled on her nipple while he thrust deep. Time seemed to stop as her pleasure expanded to fill the world. She threw her hips upward and held still. She convulsed around his thick cock. Sensation moved through her in flowing waves, so strong she almost fainted.

She'd never experienced a climax of such intensity. She squeezed her eyes shut, enjoying the ebbing arcs of satisfaction.

Ryus moved faster. Sweat beaded his forehead. Surely the wonderful orgasm still pulsing through her would detonate his climax. She squeezed her muscles around his throbbing cock, sensing how close he was…

A chime sounded. "Primus Ryus?" The soft voice of the computer.

Ryus stopped moving. "Busy, Belmarra! Go away!"

"Your pardon, Primus. Your orders were to alert you immediately to trouble on the Agricultural Level."

Ryus groaned. *Trouble on the Agricultural Level.* Years ago, he'd instructed Belmarra to use those words if Popo escaped.

The *patitou*, Arooa's beloved pet. The little animal had never wandered free. His heart overturned. She might come to harm without her protective cage.

He withdrew from Snow's sweet channel, knowing he'd never be able to climax with this on his mind. "Sorry," he whispered, touching her face.

Her eyes shone with tears. "You're the one who missed out, not me," she murmured. Her soft cheeks were still pink with sensual ardor.

The Council resembled males who had lived through a mass-duel. How difficult it must have been, watching him enjoy what was still denied to them. If only he could have finished.

He'd been so close.

Rising, he opened the drawer under the bed. Like all such drawers it held cleansing towels. He handed one to Snow. Silently they cleaned and dressed themselves.

Meanwhile the Council conferred in whispers. At last Hirdos spoke. "The test was inconclusive."

Ryus strode forward aggressively, hoping they recalled his threat to fight every one of them. "Test was *interrupted*. Not my fault."

Taddus raised dark brows. "No? Even though you and Arooa brought an illegal pet aboard in the first place?"

Aghast, Ryus stared at him. When had Taddus found out about Popo? Did they all know about the pet?

"The *patitou*'s existence is immaterial," Hirdos said quickly. "Long ago the Council learned of it and decided to ignore its presence. Let's keep to the matter at hand. We have two choices—repeat the test or make our decision. Since we can't bear to undergo this temptation again, we've arrived at a decision."

Coming up behind him, Snow took his hand. *Don't worry*, he wanted to tell her. *I will never let them send you away.* He felt her fingers tremble but she faced the Council without flinching.

"Snow Jarrett," Hirdos continued, "taking into consideration Secondus Delos' assurances and our own observations today, we've decided you may participate in the Spring Running. Following the event, your new husband, whoever he may be, will be tested. If the mating was successful, the Council will take no further action. If not, when the ship makes planetfall, you will be left on Jahariz."

Snow's cold fingers clutched his. Well, it wasn't what they'd hoped for but at least they'd won a reprieve. In the time until the Spring Running, he would continue working with Snow. They would mate again and again, twice or perhaps three times per day, until her muscles were strong.

Anticipation rose in him. He squeezed her hand, pleased when she pressed back.

"Furthermore," Hirdos went on, "the Council has decided that with fifty Brides awake, we have a volatile situation on the *Ecstasy of Generations.*" Pausing, he looked sternly at Ryus. "We cannot have males choosing Brides prior to the Spring Running. That would result in arguments. Duels. *Deaths.*

"All must be done in an orderly fashion. Therefore, we will require that every male aboard take oath not to mate until the Spring Running."

Beside him, Snow gasped. Ryus' heart sank. The half-completed mating had been brief ecstasy. Now he felt like a starving male who'd been given one bite and had the rest snatched away.

"Primus Ryus," Hirdos finished, his tone formal, "you may take your oath with the Council immediately." The Council members stood.

Escape was impossible. Releasing Snow's hand, Ryus crossed his arms over his chest, resting his palms on his upper arms.

Hirdos led the oath. "Unsheathe!" he called.

Ryus' claws shot out, ten tips piercing his flesh. A red bead welled up from each of the wounds.

Asher groaned. Perhaps his claws had sunk too deep. The coppery scent of blood filled the room.

Hirdos began, "By my claws, I swear—"

The other males spoke together. "*By my claws, I swear—*"

"Not to mate with any Bride until the Spring Running, on pain of the Council's most severe punishment—"

"Most severe punishment—" they echoed.

His tone dire, Hirdos concluded, "Gelding."

Chapter Six

Ryus walked Snow back to her cabin, hating to leave her but knowing he must put distance between them quickly. He had to search for the lost *patitou*. That was his duty now.

The scent of her arousal lingered, forcing him to relive those ecstatic moments when he'd been inside her, giving her pleasure, striving for his own release. He fought his raging desire to back Snow against the wall, raise her tunic and finish their interrupted mating.

By my claws, I swear...

Silently he cursed the Council.

"Gelding," she said. "Does that mean what I think it does? If you broke your vow, the Council would actually remove your testicles?"

Grimly he touched his right shoulder. "Traditional punishment for certain grave offenses."

"That's barbaric! I thought you people were civilized!"

"How do your people punish criminals?" he asked.

"Confinement with other criminals. Loss of freedom to come and go as they please. They're penned together like—like animals." She gazed up at him curiously. "Strange—I can't think of a word for it."

"Our culture *has* no such place." He shuddered. "Most Terilians would rather lose their sexual function than their freedom."

"We Earthians have so much to learn about your society." She sighed. "What was all that about an illegal pet?"

He explained to her about the *patitou*. "Going to look for her. Hopefully if I call her she'll come to me."

Snow's expression brightened. "I'll tag along. I want to see the agricultural area."

"Not a good idea." Alone with her on the private Agricultural Level? Before long he'd be urging her down onto the fragrant grass and mounting her. No male could resist such temptation. His testicles tightened, drawing close against his body as he imagined the punishment that would follow.

"But I want to help," she said.

"Snow, you heard the oath." Agony twisted through his gut. "Have to avoid each other now."

"What do you mean?"

"My need for you is barely controllable. My body is screaming to complete our mating." He closed his eyes for a moment in pain. "Need to stay away from you."

"I can't see you at all?" The hurt in her voice broke his heart. "Until when?"

"Until the Spring Running." Could he endure her absence for so many days?

He would have to endure. He couldn't trust himself when he was close to her. Only by staying away from her could he avoid the Council's punishment.

They'd reached her cabin at last. Her back to the door, she looked up at him, her expression mutinous. "We can't even sit together—just to talk—like friends?"

"Not unless you want to see me gelded." Hands shaking, he leaned forward and rubbed his face against hers one last time, marking her with his scent. "Farewell, little one."

* * * * *

After Ryus left, Snow went to Sick Bay. She found Dr. Delos in his office, speaking with the ship's computer. He broke off when he saw her and invited her to take a seat.

She perched on a stool, wishing she and Ryus could have consummated their mating. In spite of the incredibly beautiful orgasm he'd given her, she felt unfulfilled. He hadn't climaxed. The act was incomplete.

The slight soreness of her nipples made her recall how he'd sucked them while the Council watched. Her pussy clenched with longing. How could she bear Ryus' absence until the Spring Running?

"Hirdos contacted me a few moments ago," Delos said. "So the mating test was inconclusive."

She sighed with exasperation. "Everything seemed to be going well. If only we hadn't been interrupted, it would have been successful."

"I'm afraid your readings say otherwise." He frowned. "In my opinion, you were fortunate the test ended prematurely."

She fell silent, stunned by the certainty in his tone. Her own doctor had expected her to fail. Cold shivers ran down her back, dousing her desire. If she'd failed, she'd have had to leave the ship.

She'd have had to leave Ryus.

"I'll have another chance at the Spring Running," she said. "I've been doing the therapy—with Ryus and by myself. But what if it's not enough? Isn't there anything else I can do?"

The doctor studied her for a long moment. His professional gaze seemed to examine not only her face and limbs but her strength, courage and will.

"There *is* something else," she guessed. Her heart beat wildly. "Tell me."

"I'm not sure you can endure the procedure."

Lifting her chin, she met his troubled eyes. "Whatever it is, I'll do it."

At last he rose from his stool. "Come with me."

* * * * *

Hoping the *patitou* would have returned to its familiar environment, Ryus went to the cave first. He crouched down by the empty cage, noting there was still food in her bowl. Arooa would have been distraught at the creature's escape. Popo had been her last link with her family on Teril.

Just as Popo was *his* last link with Arooa.

No doubt he'd been careless when he'd last fed the *patitou*. He must have left the cage door unlatched. His mind had been entirely on Snow while he forgot his obligations.

He circled the area around the cave three times, spreading out in a wider radius during each lap of the search. Checking in with Belmarra, she assured him that none of her cameras had caught the animal's image. "I can't see under the soil," she added. "On Teril, wild *patitous* live in dens."

"Know that." His response trailed off into a growl. The Agricultural Level went on for miles. If the *patitou* had burrowed underground, he'd never find her.

He walked for hours, scanning the soil, calling Popo's name. Once he was away from the acrid odor concentrated in the cave, he expected to pick up the animal's scent. But he couldn't trace her. She must have gone underground, yet he couldn't find any soil disturbed by digging.

The area was laced with canals that brought water for the walking sprinklers. Could Popo have drowned in a canal?

Despair weighed his shoulders down, slowed his steps. Maybe his activity was frightening her away. Forcing himself to relax, he sat under a tree, his back against the trunk. The glaring artificial sunlight hurt his eyes, so he closed them. If he stayed motionless, Popo would come to him. She would. She *must*.

Now that he was still, images of Snow flooded his mind. He wanted to see her again and yet he dreaded it. How could he be near her and yet keep his vow? If he continued to supervise her therapy, he'd have to do it through the ship's computer.

A mere touch of Snow's tempting, smooth skin and his body would surge with uncontrollable desire. But could he sit in her cabin, across the room perhaps? Just to talk with her would be blissful. He loved watching her changeable expressions when he spoke of Teril. The eager light in her eyes seduced him more thoroughly than her lovely breasts or her delightful, rounded buttocks that were made for a male's caress.

For *his* caress.

What a miracle that she trusted him, as though they were a mated couple and not two different species, one of whom had kidnapped the other.

A sick feeling crept into his gut. How had this Earth female become so important to him, so quickly? Hadn't he sworn to himself that even if he took another wife, she would never usurp Arooa's place in his heart?

Would it be better to choose *another* Bride at the Spring Running? Someone to use for bodily release, without falling into the snare of love? That way he could guard his wife's memory forever.

The sound of something brushing against leaves snapped his eyes open. He scented the air, straining to tease out Popo's scent. Then he saw what had made the noise—a flying *gotharz*, one of the warty insects that pollinated plants. Disappointed, he swore under his breath.

He had always been careful to set the cage's latch. Suppose someone else had opened the cage? Someone who wanted to interrupt Snow's test? Someone who wanted Snow to fail?

He called out to the computer. "Belmarra? Did Durin come to the Agricultural Level after he left the Council meeting?"

"I cannot answer questions about another primus' past whereabouts. Providing this information would violate Durin's right of privacy."

"Never mind. I'll ask him myself."

"Is that wise?"

Ignoring the computer's question, he leapt to his feet and stalked off to find his enemy.

* * * * *

"I suppose Ryus is looking for Popo right now," the doctor said as he led Snow through the corridors of Sick Bay.

"So Hirdos told you about the pet's escape?" Snow looked up at him in surprise. "Ryus said Popo's presence on the ship is a secret."

Delos gave her his gentle smile. "Ryus' wife was a doctor. I worked with her for years. I know all about Popo."

"I hope Ryus finds her. He's awfully worried."

"I'm sure she'll come to no harm," the doctor said, his tone soothing. He punched a code into a control panel. A door slid open, revealing a small room containing a long, gleaming metal box. Tubes entered it at either end. "Look, Snow. You spent your first six weeks on the ship in this *Walzinia* chamber."

She stared at the frightening box in dismay. "I wasn't lying on a bed, like all the other Brides?"

"Your severe illness merited special treatment. And it worked. When I woke you, your strength was much improved."

Snow nodded. "I'm amazed I was able to walk right away."

"That was due to this chamber. When you lie inside it, you're bombarded by *vosin* rays, which create miniscule tears in your muscles. As the tears heal, your muscles strengthen."

"So if I get inside that ugly thing again, I'll keep improving?"

Dr. Delos touched his right shoulder. "At double the rate of ordinary physical therapy. But I warn you, the process will be painful. You were heavily sedated after you were taken from Earth. That's why you don't remember the agony of the chamber."

"But I still need crutches to walk! I think you took me out too soon."

Apparently Delos liked criticism of his medical judgment no more than any Earth doctor. His brows drew together. "I woke you when I did—earlier than the other Brides—because the level of sedatives in your blood was dangerously high. Your body has not yet expelled all the drugs. If you return to the chamber, you will have to endure the rays without sedation."

Snow hesitated, looking at the coffin-like object. Could she endure the pain? These Terilian males were tough—she'd seen enough of them to know that much. If Dr. Delos used the word *agony*, she could be sure he meant it.

But she needed to be strong enough to stay on the ship. Strong enough to mate with Ryus. Strong enough to be his wife.

"You think I didn't go through some horrific medical treatments on Earth?" She lifted her chin. "When can I start?"

Chapter Seven

꼉

Ryus found Durin on the Exercise and Recreation Level, sparring with a tall secondus. Gazing into the fight-pen through one of the viewports, he watched the secondus leap at Durin, who spun out of reach then darted back instantly. With a lightning-quick under-slash, Durin scored "first cut" against his opponent. The secondus fell back, his chest blooming red from the dye on the sparring gloves.

Ryus had almost forgotten how fast Durin moved. The anticipation of battle rose in his blood. Involuntarily his claws shot out.

He banged his palm against the control panel. The door slid open. The game computer intoned, "Match interrupted."

Durin and his secondus partner whirled around to see who had committed the breach of etiquette.

"Get out," Ryus told the secondus, jerking his head toward the doorway.

"We haven't finished," the secondus protested. Ryus growled and raised one hand. His razor-sharp claws caught the light.

Losing his nerve, the secondus fled the fight-pen.

Durin stood his ground. "I suppose you're angry that I brought my concerns about Snow Jarrett to the Council," he said.

"Should have challenged me like a primus, not avenged yourself on Snow."

"It's not all about *you*, Ryus. I want the Spring Running to be successful—for everyone."

Ryus advanced on him, hatred coursing through his veins. He could barely wait to smell the other male's blood. "What did you do with Arooa's *patitou*?"

"I had nothing to do with the pet's escape."

Furious at the lie, Ryus raised both arms in combat-ready position. "Take off your gloves."

"You're insane. If we injure each other, we'll miss the Spring Running. Is that truly what you want?"

A low growl broke from Ryus' throat. *"What did you do with Popo?"*

"I told you, nothing!"

A red haze filled Ryus' sight. Durin cared neither for the *patitou*'s safety nor for Snow's fate. All he wanted was revenge. For that he deserved to be hurt, to be slashed and bloodied.

Yet honor required that he be given one more chance. "Will you swear by the Great Fur-Mother?"

"How dare you challenge my spoken truth!" Stripping off his sparring gloves, Durin flung them to the floor.

"Ready?" Ryus demanded.

His opponent lifted his upper lip, revealing his gleaming fangs. The message had been given—*I'm ready to fight*.

Rage dammed further words. In one smooth movement Ryus crouched and leapt. Durin sprang forward at the same moment. They grappled in midair, then dashed apart as they landed.

They'd both drawn blood. Durin's chest was marked. Ryus' shoulder bled from a deep wound. He didn't feel the pain of it yet. It made no difference anyway. He would punish his enemy.

They circled each other at a half crouch. Ryus knew his opponent expected a quick attack, so he waited. Durin leapt and Ryus dodged aside. Encountering no resistance, Durin hit the floor. Ryus whirled and followed him down.

They grappled again, rolling on the ground while Ryus desperately tried to pin his opponent. Remembering how long it had taken to defeat Durin in their previous encounter, he redoubled his efforts. This had to be resolved quickly, because any minute now —

The door slid open. Two security seconduses rushed in, weapons drawn. "Desist immediately," the white-haired one commanded, "or you'll get a dose from this Mind-Bender."

Ryus shuddered, having no desire to spend the next few days as a drooling idiot, singing to himself and picking imaginary insects out of his hair. Nevertheless he tried to bluff it out.

"Leave us!" he replied. "Primus business here." Releasing Durin, he leapt to his feet.

"Security has no jurisdiction to interfere in a challenge," Durin growled, rising as though every bone in his body hurt.

"This is *not* a legal, registered challenge," the security secondus answered coldly. "Accompany us to Sick Bay — before we lose patience."

Seeing no alternative, Ryus strode off toward Sick Bay, trying to look as though he had nothing to do with the security seconduses at his heels.

Beside him, Durin spoke unexpectedly. "I didn't go to the Council to get revenge on you."

Ryus gave him a quick, surprised glance. Could he trust the other male's words? He had doubts...yet Durin's voice radiated sincerity.

"Then why?" he demanded.

Durin hesitated, looking at the security seconduses. They dropped back a few paces.

Durin lowered his voice. "When we fought the first time...I understand why you challenged me back then. It's true that I pursued other men's wives. I did that because — because my own wife was unable to satisfy me."

"Phauru?" He remembered her well, a sweet-faced female with orange-striped hair. "Was something wrong with her?"

"She had an illness similar to Snow Jarrett's. Secondus Galzin was treating her but none of the medications worked—she had an unusual genetic structure." Durin looked down, his face working. "You think these last two years have been a horror? All our females dead, no one to mate with? Imagine having a wife whose every word, every gesture, makes you want to mount her. Yet when you do, her weakness prevents—" His voice broke.

With this confession, much became clear. Durin's distasteful actions. His brother Taddus' refusal to chastise him.

"How long have you gone without mating?" Ryus asked. "Three years? Four?" Was Durin closer to death than the rest of them?

"Two years, the same as everyone else. After you and I battled, my brother decided my problem must be resolved. At his request, his wife mated with me."

Ryus sucked in his breath. "Kind of her," he managed to say.

Durin tapped his right shoulder. "Vervina was an admirable female... Anyway, after I met Snow Jarrett in Sick Bay, Taddus showed me her medical report. I couldn't bear the thought of a male choosing her at the Spring Running, then being unable to climax. Not after two years of this terrible celibacy. No one deserves that kind of torture."

"Snow will do fine." He believed that. He *had* to believe that.

"I suppose you mean to choose her at the Running." Durin looked at him expectantly.

Ryus didn't reply. He'd borne his sorrow for two years, the pain like a claw in his heart. Now with the added burden of his feelings for Snow, the claw was slashing his heart in two.

"Take this as a well-meant warning," Durin said. "Being married to a female who can't satisfy you is a fate I wouldn't wish on my worst enemy." With a short, unhumorous laugh, he added, "Not even you."

A thrill of dread crawled down Ryus' spine. "Won't matter if she's exiled to Jahariz."

"Despite what Hirdos thinks, I'm *not* heartless. It pains me to think of leaving the female behind. But what is best for the ship?" His voice vibrated with passion. "For all of us?"

Ryus answered sternly, "We can't do right by all of us unless we act morally toward each one of us."

Durin didn't reply but his expression turned thoughtful.

They'd reached Sick Bay. Extracting promises from them not to resume their duel, the security seconduses left. Durin strode off to another part of Sick Bay while Belmarra directed Ryus to a private cubicle.

He found Delos seated beside a still-sedated Janis Stone, holding her hand. Ryus gave his friend a skeptical look as the doctor jumped to his feet.

"Foolish to choose a female you won't be able to marry," Ryus commented.

Delos' eyebrows rose. "*That's* the sapphire calling the ocean blue. Why don't *you* let Snow go into exile and pick another Bride?"

"That better be a rhetorical question." Ryus gestured at his shoulder. "Feel like patching me up?"

With a last reluctant glance toward Janis, Delos led him to a healing room and tended the wound. "I suppose Durin gave you this? Who won?"

"Security interrupted us."

"Good."

"Good?" Ryus said, outraged.

"Haven't we lost enough shipmates already?" The doctor finished by handing him a vial. Ryus opened the stopper and sniffed. The agony of his wound faded.

"Secondus Delos?" Belmarra's voice echoed through the small room. "You asked for an alert when Snow's pain level reaches 5.9. That has just occurred."

"Acknowledged." Delos clapped Ryus on his unhurt shoulder. "You're free to go."

Alarmed, Ryus followed him from the room. "What are you doing to Snow?"

"She's in the *Walzinia* chamber."

Nausea snaked through his gut. "Unsedated?" Knowing where the chamber was kept, he bounded down the corridor, leaving Delos behind.

When the door opened he rushed into the room, staring down at her through the chamber's clear cover. Snow's hands were gripped together. Sweat beaded her forehead. Glistening tracks of tears on her flushed cheeks made his heart overturn.

The *vosin* rays activated. The chamber glowed blue, the color of death. Snow's white tunic abruptly turned into the deep cobalt that clothed a corpse.

She's dead. He stopped breathing. *I'll never hold her again. Never mate with her. Never be her husband.* Sorrow engulfed him, nearly pulling him under.

Her features twisted. She raised white-knuckled fists to cover her face.

Heart crashing against his chest, Ryus fumbled with the controls, unable to manage the sequence. Terror made his fingers clumsy and awkward. Cursing, he slowed his trembling hands and tried again.

At last he deactivated the chamber and threw the lid open.

Snow gazed up at him in shock as he scooped her out of the chamber, cradling her against his chest. He closed his eyes and buried his face in her fragrant curls, whispering thanks to the Great Fur-Mother that she was safe.

Delos came in, folding his arms over his chest, a disgusted expression on his face.

"What were you thinking?" Ryus demanded. "Snow was in *pain*." Fury surged through him. He badly wanted to hurt the doctor.

Snow pushed against his chest. "Put me down!" He set her on her feet. Letting go was difficult. He wanted to rush to his cabin with her, caress the shapely arms and legs that had endured long minutes of agony, keep her safe forever.

Her expression still creased with pain, she turned stiffly toward Delos. "Doctor, what happened? Did I get my full hour?"

"Forty-six minutes," Delos told her.

"I want the full hour!"

Determined not to let Snow return to the chamber, Ryus glared at the doctor. "She doesn't need this!" His right claws shot out, which relieved him only slightly. "The physical therapy—"

"Is not enough." Delos strode forward, standing nose-to-nose with him. "Sheathe your Mother-scratching claws. I don't understand why everyone's suddenly questioning my medical judgment today."

"I *forbid* this." Ryus gestured toward the chamber. "No patient should have to endure this kind of pain during therapy."

Snow's gray eyes flashed. "I asked for this treatment. I'm doing it for us." She put her hand on his arm. "I want to be strong enough to be your wife."

Torn, he gazed down at Snow's upturned face. Part of him yearned to embrace her, to tell her how much he wanted her, to assure her that he would mate with her at the Spring Running. To tell her he'd choose her as his wife...

Wife. Arooa had been his wife. His only wife.

They'd chosen each other three times. For Arooa's sake he'd braved his father's anger, his family's disapproval of his marriage to a female of the Gray-Striped Pelt.

When he didn't answer, Snow took a step back. "I'm assuming too much." Her lips had turned white. "I thought you cared for me but—"

The words rushed unbidden from his mouth. "The more I care for you, the more I feel disloyal to my wife."

He was horrified by the words as soon as they were spoken. Judging from the way the color drained from her face, the hurt he'd just inflicted on Snow was worse than the agony of the *Walzinia* chamber.

"I was always second-best with my husband," she said. "I will never go through that again." Her magnificent breasts lifted as she drew a deep breath. She'd never seemed more desirable. "I intend to be strong by the Spring Running. And I intend to have a husband who loves me. *Only me.*"

Before Ryus could form a reply, Delos stepped forward and took Snow's arm. "Come into the examining room. I need to check your vital signs. And don't worry—you *will* be strong," he assured her as he led her away. "At the Running, males will be fighting over you. You might even marry a Council member. Hirdos himself was talking about choosing you…" The doctor's cruelly cheerful voice trailed off as the door slid shut behind them.

Ryus realized anger was of no use. He'd brought this on himself. Nevertheless he gritted his teeth as he paced back and forth, waiting for them to return. He'd walk Snow back to her cabin. He'd apologize. He'd explain.

When the door finally reopened, Delos came in alone. The doctor regarded him in silence for a long moment.

"Where's Snow?" Ryus demanded.

"She returned to her cabin. And don't try to enter it. At her request, I changed the door admittance function to keep you out."

Ryus' heart plummeted. How could he talk to Snow if she refused to see him? "Thought we were friends," he accused the doctor.

"I *am* your friend." Delos strode closer. "And as your friend, let me tell you this. You were offered a second chance at happiness by a lovely, intelligent female. And what did you do? Drove her away with your stubborn inability to let go of the past."

"Can't help the way I feel." Fury and confusion spun together in his mind.

"Stop wallowing in grief." Delos put his hand on Ryus' arm. How did he dare? Didn't the doctor know how badly he wanted to slash something to pieces? "Ry, we can't build a new civilization if we're always looking backward. There's no point in going on with this venture without wives."

Gritting his teeth, Ryus pulled away. "Know that. But I left Teril *because* of Arooa. My Peltdom never accepted her."

Delos brushed that aside with a wave of his hand. "Most of us left for similar reasons. Teril was too structured, too hidebound. That's why this venture is worth our sweat and toil—even though our Terilian wives are gone." He fixed Ryus with a stern look. "Would Arooa want you to mourn her forever? Or would she want you to be happy?"

The doctor's words washed over him. He couldn't deny the truth. Arooa had always put him first.

Just as he'd put her first.

"Think about it," Delos concluded. "Think *hard*. In the meantime, come with me."

Ryus followed him down a corridor, figuring Del was about to assign some of the newly awakened Brides to him for treatment. While the females had received various forms of nerve and muscle stimulation during their medically induced comas, no doubt some of them would need physical therapy. Perhaps he could work with them in large groups and recruit some of the orderlies to help. While most of his shipmates would envy his chance to work with the Brides, it meant little to him. The only female he cared about was Snow.

He hoped Del would instruct him quickly. Snow's disappointed face lingered in his mind. His need to talk to her was rapidly growing desperate.

As they entered one of the research laboratories, a high-pitched voice squeaked, "Ryus! Ryus!"

Joyously he rushed to the cage and freed Popo. She ran up his arm and snuggled against his neck. Never before had he been so happy to breathe in her acrid odor, to feel her soft fur against his skin.

Turning, he asked, "Del, where did you find her?" Something about the doctor's smug expression revealed the truth. "You had her all along!"

He'd accused Durin of a deed he'd never committed. Grimacing, he realized he owed Durin an apology.

"I had to interrupt the mating test somehow," Delos said. "Snow needed more time."

The explanation quenched his anger. He couldn't say whether or not the mating would have failed. But if it had, Snow would already be sentenced to exile.

"Thanks." Delos' action had given Snow more time to build her strength. "But why didn't you tell me about Popo earlier? Know how many hours I spent looking for this little furball?" Popo climbed up his hair and nibbled on his ear. Wincing, he brought her down.

"Unbelievable as it may sound, I have other concerns aside from you and Snow. Including fifty newly awakened Brides who are frightened and upset."

"Feared Popo was hurt." Ryus adjusted the front of his tunic to make a carrying space for the little creature.

Delos raised a skeptical eyebrow. "Hurt? A *patitou* is perfectly safe on this ship. None of her natural enemies are aboard." With a dismissive wave of his hand, he added, "Get her out of my laboratory, will you? I can't stand the odor."

With one hand over Popo's quivering fur, Ryus left Sick Bay and used the jumps to reach the Agricultural Level. Soon the *patitou* was back in her cage, eating from her bowl contentedly. He couldn't help smiling as he watched.

Until she looked up at him, her beady eyes bright. "Rooa? Rooa?"

"Not coming back," he muttered. Her gaze showed no comprehension. The *patitou* could not understand complex ideas.

Lifting her out of the cage again, he walked out of the cave and knelt in the grass.

Delos had spoken the truth. Arooa had always wanted him to be happy.

The first time he'd seen Snow, he'd been struck by how much Arooa would have liked her. He'd recalled how his wife had valued courage above all other virtues.

Today Snow had proved she had as much courage as any male he'd ever fought. He clenched his fists, trying to shut out the agony she'd faced in the *Walzinia* chamber.

She'd done that for him. *I want to be strong enough to be your wife.* Drawing a deep breath, he wondered, *Am I worthy of that kind of effort?*

He tried to imagine standing aside while another male mated with her, became her husband. The mere thought made his pulse hammer with rage.

Snow was right. She needed a male who would put her first. Not treat her as a pale replacement of his first wife. She was an alluring female who deserved the full attention of a loving, caring mate.

The *patitou* tickled his neck. He brought her down, cradling her in his palms.

A memory, however treasured, couldn't provide companionship, couldn't stand by his side when danger threatened, couldn't build a new life with him on a new world.

With a heavy sigh, he gazed up at the metal-sheathed ceiling, painted violet to resemble the sky of Teril. He had to lock Arooa away in his memory. Not forget her—never that—but learn to live without her.

He'd made a start when he fell in love with Snow.

He set the *patitou* on the grass, close to a flowering *ritilla*. She lifted her snout, caught the scent and ran forward. When she settled in to nibble at the plant, he stood.

Closing his eyes, he whispered, "Farewell."

He left the Agricultural Level without looking back.

Chapter Eight

ಐ

"Bride Snow?" Belmarra's low-pitched voice insinuated itself through Snow's cabin. "Primus Ryus is at your door again."

Snow gritted her teeth. "Please tell him I can't see him."

"This is the twentieth time in eleven days that he has tried to contact you."

"Really? I thought this was number nineteen."

Apparently sarcasm was beyond Belmarra's abilities, for she answered calmly, "Twenty. Would you like a complete listing of the attempted contacts?"

"No. New instructions. Do not let me know when Ryus tries to contact me." Each time it was a stronger temptation to hurry to the door, rush into his arms and lead him inside. "Just tell him I don't want to see him or talk to him."

"Instructions accepted."

"Good!" After all, she'd learned her lesson with her ex-husband, Craig. She'd never come first with him. He'd always regretted the breakup with his old girlfriend. Karin had been his ideal woman, he'd told Snow…repeatedly.

Maybe that's why their marriage hadn't been strong enough to endure when she'd become ill.

Any historian knew that history repeated itself. Only a fool fell into the trap of making the same mistake over and over.

She had enough to think about without worrying about her ridiculous infatuation with Ryus. All the Brides were awake now. Their liaison to the Terilians, Janis Stone, had convinced the Council to hold a huge wedding. Snow herself was on three committees to plan it, including one to document everything with detailed written descriptions.

She was thrilled to have the companionship of other Earth women and happy to be kept busy with the committee work. Hectic days were punctuated by nearly unbearable bouts of muscle stimulation in the *Walzinia* chamber. Each day she got through the session by promising herself she would never return to Sick Bay. But each day saw her returning for one more agonizing treatment.

Secondus Delos seemed pleased with her results. She no longer wore crutches. She walked, jumped and ran as though she'd never been ill. Every day she rose from her bed with ease, thankful to have escaped the nursing home.

All this kept her from dwelling too much on her failed relationship with Ryus. Sleep-cycles were the worst time, because during them, memories assailed her relentlessly. She imagined his hands caressing her nipples, gently stroking until they peaked. His body on top of hers…his hard cock pressed against her stomach…

She could suppress those thoughts but she couldn't prevent the dreams that tortured her. Every night she relived the mating test, feeling again the consuming joy when he first pushed inside her, the wonderful thrusts of his powerful cock. She usually woke with tears on her cheeks.

He doesn't love you. Forget him. You'll find another mate.

But she didn't want anyone else. Only Ryus.

* * * * *

"All Brides report to the fourteenth floor. Follow the blinking corridor lights to the central elevators. All Brides…"

The Earth women flocked into the corridors. Snow swore under her breath as her cabin door swished shut behind her. The announcement had interrupted a glorious dream. Ryus kneeling between her parted thighs, giving her overwhelming pleasure with his warm, wet tongue…

Coming out of the cabin next to Snow's, Valida looked at her curiously. Over the last few days, they'd sat together at meals and quickly become friends.

"Your face is flushed," Valida said. "What's wrong?"

"I'd tell you but then I'd have to kill you," Snow teased, not wanting to admit to erotic dreams.

"Maybe we're being called for the Spring Running." The other woman's dusky cheeks darkened with a sudden blush. "I was having this incredible dream. I'm too embarrassed to talk about it." Her brown eyes apprehensive, she added, "I hope I'm ready for a Terilian husband."

Snow patted her friend's shoulder. "Don't be afraid. I'm sure you'll find someone nice."

When they reached the Agricultural Level, the Council awaited them. As soon as all the Brides were present, Council member Goldus rose.

"Beautiful Brides, welcome to one of the most important events of the Terilian people. You may have noticed yourself experiencing intense erotic longings recently. You're merely responding to our male pheromones and to your own desires to mate during today's Spring Running."

Looking toward the Council, Snow happened to catch Hirdos' eye. For a long moment their gazes locked. His intent expression told her that the doctor's words were true—Hirdos desired her.

Her breasts ached to be fondled by a male's big hands. Her nipples peaked as her desire mounted. She reached one hand inside her tunic and ran her fingertips over one stiffened peak, barely stifling a moan.

Hirdos' eyes widened.

Her pussy pulsed, heavy and hot with arousal. Soon she would be mating with a Terilian.

Would it be Ryus? She remembered the question he'd posed weeks ago. *Should I participate in something I believe is wrong?* Perhaps he wouldn't attend the Spring Running.

Her stomach dropped and some of her excitement died.

Surely he would be sensible and find a Bride, rather than risk death.

Goldus continued, "When the whistle sounds, run deep into the park and conceal yourselves. At the end of twenty minutes, the secondus-ranked males will search for you. Don't make it too easy for them, Brides! Part of the joy of the Spring Running is the challenge of finding you before mating."

Would Ryus try to find her? Or would he choose another?

Ryus mating with another Bride…a pang of agony worse than the *vosin* rays knifed through her.

"After another hour, the fifty primus-ranked males will be allowed into the park," Goldus said. "Be aware that primuses have first choice among females, so even if you've already mated with a secondus, you may still be fortunate enough to gain a primus husband."

A primus husband. Ryus?

Goldus concluded, "May the Great Fur-Mother bless us all today. Brides, good Running."

The whistle sounded. The crowd of women surged forward into the park.

"Run, ladies!" a woman shouted, far ahead. The Brides at the front of the crowd obeyed. Soon the whole group was running.

Snow fell into an easy jog. She looked for Valida but they'd become separated by the crowd. She hoped the Running would go well for her friend.

She thought briefly of the nursing home. Only a few weeks ago she'd been more helpless than a newborn baby, unable to feed herself. Now her legs were powerful. A boulder loomed in her path. Without thinking she leapt, clearing it effortlessly. Her heart skipped with joy.

Ryus had helped her achieve this new strength. Powerful enough to intimidate other males, he was simultaneously gentle and encouraging.

And a wonderful lover.

She ached with need. She'd never be happy until his palms caressed her thighs again, moving their way slowly upward. Shivering with arousal, she recalled his fingers stroking her curls.

She mustn't let sexual desire distract her from her plan.

Dr. Delos had let it slip that the Spring Running would be held in this area. Several days ago she'd come here alone, observing the long grass in the park, the acres of crops, the walking sprinklers and the canals from which they drew water.

She'd asked the doctor whether anyone swam in the canals. Shocked, he'd replied that no Terilian liked swimming.

But he'd assured her that the water in the canals was pure and fresh.

The crowd thinned out. Some women concealed themselves behind boulders or in trees. One woman climbed high then called out, "I see the Terilians!"

The secondus males were on their way.

Snow changed direction, running west toward the crops. Soon she found a canal. Five feet wide, six feet deep, the water inside was clear and sparkling. Seating herself on the edge, she hesitated for just a moment, then removed her tunic and shoes.

She slipped in, laughing with pleasure as the cool water flowed over her naked body, buoying her up. She'd always loved swimming. Holding her breath, she dunked her head under, then raised her face, shaking her wet curls back.

Her scent was concealed by the water. She didn't want a secondus mate. She wanted Ryus. *If* he wanted her as well.

The canal had a swift current, no doubt designed that way to keep the water from becoming stagnant. She let it carry her along.

A throaty sound made her stop. She held onto the edge of the canal, peering out through the tall, fernlike plants that lined each side of the waterway.

One of the Brides was already mating with a Terilian. He was a big fellow, almost as large as Ryus. Standing, he held the woman in his arms. Her legs were tight around his waist, her arms surrounding his neck. As he thrust into her, she threw her head back, letting her hair swing free. An incoherent sound of pleasure burst from her throat.

He bent his head, nibbling her neck. She cried out again and he groaned.

Despite the cool water, Snow's pussy pulsed with heat. Forcing herself to turn away, she resumed floating, letting her eyes drift shut.

After a few minutes she heard the sound of running feet.

A male with glossy black hair raced after a chubby red-haired woman. He was naked, his erect cock held against his body with a red cord. The woman looked back over her shoulder, laughing when he caught her hand.

"Lovely," he said, stroking the woman's face.

"Lovely? *Me*?" she asked. Her eager gaze moved swiftly over the handsome male's muscular form.

"Your face and body are beautiful but your scent is beyond compare." He pulled at her tunic, exposing her plump breasts. Staring at them, he fell silent.

Snow remembered the first time Ryus had looked at her naked breasts, her delighted response when he touched her. Her nipples always peaked immediately at the gentle touch of his questing tongue.

Her hand crept to her mound, stroking her wet curls. Ah, if only it were Ryus touching her.

The red-haired woman said uneasily, "I know they're too droopy."

"No!" Reverently, the male covered the woman's breasts with his palms. His hands moved, rubbing her until she cried out, "Oh, that feels so good!"

God, I need Ryus. Snow slid underwater again, taking out her frustration by frog-kicking her legs, propelling herself forward.

The hour between the admittance of the seconduses and the primuses seemed to take days. At last she peered out and spotted the dark-haired orderly she'd seen in Sick Bay. The jeweled band in his hair proclaimed his primus status. He lifted his face, his nostrils flaring. Had he scented her? She was relieved when he began running in the opposite direction.

The primuses are here. She quivered with excitement. Was Ryus searching for her?

Then she saw him in the distance, running side by side with another male, heading straight for her. As they drew closer, she realized the golden-haired male beside him was Hirdos.

They wore identical red cords around their erect penises. Hirdos' cock was even longer than Ryus' but not as thick.

She held onto the edge of the canal, gazing toward them. "I didn't think you'd find me so quickly," she called.

"Come out of the water." Ryus knelt at the side of the canal, pushing past tall fronds to offer his hands. "Belmarra told us where you were."

"Isn't that cheating?" She let him help her out of the canal. Water ran off her body in long, sparkling rivulets. The two males stared at her, eyes wide.

"Primus privilege," Hirdos said at last, licking his lips. "By the great Fur-Mother, I've never seen such beauty."

Ryus drew her close. "Torture, not being with you all those days. Want to apologize. Hate myself for hurting you."

"Don't hate yourself," she whispered, reveling in the feel of his broad chest. "I missed you." Her pussy pulsed. With two aroused males this close, her body yearned for release.

The longing was swiftly growing unbearable. She wanted to sink to the ground and part her legs. She needed Ryus' cock inside her, thrusting deep and fast.

"Won't ever forget Arooa. But I've accepted that she's gone." His voice dropped. "Mate with me. I swear you won't be sorry."

Hirdos took a step closer. "Not so fast, Ry." Reaching out, he caressed Snow's cheek. "I know you're fond of him. But if you mate with *me*, you'll be a Council member's wife."

"*If* I'm strong enough for a successful mating," Snow said.

He touched his right shoulder, looking away.

She knew which one she wanted. She opened her lips to speak.

Ryus' arms tightened around her. "Wait, Snow. Both of us desire you. To settle the dispute, Hirdos and I will fight."

"No! I don't want either of you to be hurt." She looked from him to Hirdos. "Isn't there any other way? Why can't I choose?"

The two males consulted by glance. "You can," Ryus said, his deep voice reluctant. "Tradition is, you let both of us pleasure you. Then you make your choice."

"Oh!" She licked her lips. "What exactly will you do to me?"

Hirdos' hot gaze swept over her body. "We'll both bring you to orgasm without intercourse. You'll make your choice then mate with the victor."

The smoldering arousal she'd felt since her dream burst into flames. She grinned. "What are we waiting for?"

Chapter Nine

Snow lay on her back in the tall grass, luxuriating in the heat of the artificial lights beaming down from the false sky. As Ryus stretched out to her left, she grabbed his hand. "Are you all right with this?" she asked softly.

"It's our way. Barely suppressed anger creased his forehead. "Remember how I told you this is an in-between time? Once you're my wife, if another male touches you, I'll kill him."

"Don't assume she'll choose you," Hirdos said, lying on her right. "When Snow experiences the pleasure I give her, she'll choose me."

A growl was Ryus' only answer.

Hirdos brought his palm down the side of her body, starting with her chest and going slowly to her hip, making her shiver. "How strange it feels, caressing a wet female. Whatever made you immerse yourself in water?"

She breathed him in, deciding that his aroused scent reminded her of newly mown grass. "I figured the water would hide my scent from the seconduses. I wanted to wait for Ryus."

Ryus' golden eyes brightened at her words. "You need to be dry before anything else," he said. "Can't be healthy for you to be wet like this."

She giggled. How silly to think that being wet in this near-tropical heat would harm anyone. But when he and Hirdos began licking the water from her body, she stopped laughing and sighed with contentment.

The touch of their rough tongues was as relaxing as a massage, yet far more arousing. They worked in tandem, each of them licking the water from her arms then moving to her breasts. Her breathing quickened as both males sucked her nipples for long, enthralling moments.

Her nipples darkened and puckered under their sensual attention.

She needed fingers or a tongue in her pussy. Her hips jerked restlessly. She was so close to an orgasm. If only one of them would touch her clit, she'd go off like a Roman candle.

Instead they left her breasts, moving downward to her legs. Why weren't they licking the very wettest part of her — her gushing pussy?

"Patience, little one," Ryus murmured. "When you're dry, I'll pleasure you." His tongue swirled over her thighs, making her tremble with longing.

"*We'll* pleasure you," Hirdos corrected. He cradled her calf in his warm palm, alternately teasing with his lips and licking with his tongue. When the two males nuzzled her ankles and sucked her toes, her anticipation reached nearly unbearable heights. She shut her lips tightly, so tempted to beg them for an orgasm.

Hirdos stroked her cheek. "Delos told us about a new Earthian technique for sexual stimulation. *Kissing.* Will you kiss me, Snow?"

Hoping it would distract from her frenzied need, she turned on her side. She put her hand on Hirdos' shoulder and brought her lips to his. His mouth was unmoving under hers until she licked his upper lip. He flinched.

She drew away. "Relax," she murmured. "Open your mouth."

He obeyed and she kissed him again. For a moment it was as awkward as a first kiss in junior high. Then he seemed to catch the trick of it. His warm lips shifted under hers. She slid her tongue over his, withdrew, then did it again.

He groaned. She moved back, asking, "Did you like kissing?"

"By the Great Fur-Mother, it makes me want to mate!" He rolled onto his back, breathing hard.

"My turn," Ryus said, his insistent hands turning her to face him. More aggressive than Hirdos, he brought his lips to hers immediately. His mouth stroked hers, urging her lips to open. She parted them and slid her tongue against his. He surprised her again by sucking it. Her pulse quickened. Had he received detailed instructions about the art of kissing from his friend Delos?

But then, Ryus always seemed to know what he was doing.

His hand on her breast, he teased her nipple with his thumb. His tongue thrust against hers in the rhythm of intercourse while his thumb circled her peaking nipple again and again. Her stomach clenched as her arousal built.

Behind her, Hirdos stroked her cleft with eager fingers. She trembled under the soft, exciting caress. Why was his touch so light? She wanted him to thrust his fingers inside her throbbing channel.

She loved Ryus, she had no doubt about that. So was it wrong to enjoy the carnal attentions of two males who desired her? The Spring Running had brought her to the highest peak of sexual readiness. All she wanted was to feel their hands on her, their lips moving over her, their long, hard cocks against her body.

This was not *her* idea. This was their tradition. And she planned to enjoy the hell out of it.

Absorbed in kissing Ryus, she couldn't see what Hirdos was doing. She felt him withdraw his hand. Then one finger returned, slick and wet. He slid the tip into her anus.

She gasped, feeling momentary hurt as he stretched her. Then excitement raced through her as he moved his finger in a slow circle.

Ryus' rumbling growl filled her ears. "We need to take turns. Otherwise, how can she choose between us?"

"You're right." Hirdos' voice filled with the brisk decision of one accustomed to command. "I'll go first."

Glowering, Ryus moved away. Snow wanted to say something reassuring. *Don't you know how much I love you?* But she didn't want to hurt Hirdos' feelings.

Her lips twitched. The entire Council had watched, unable to participate while Ryus attempted to mate with her. Now it was Ryus' turn to watch. Was this payback?

But when Hirdos sat up and took her hands, something sparked in his blue eyes.

She blurted out, "Why are you doing this? There are hundreds of healthy Earth women. As a primus, you have first choice."

"Your courage seduced me," he answered. "I used the *Walzinia* chamber once when I injured my thigh. I could never face that agony again. *You* entered the chamber twelve times to make yourself worthy of a Terilian mate." He squeezed her hands.

To make myself strong enough for Ryus.

"Get on with it," Ryus said, his tone ungracious. "Don't want to be late for our own weddings." He clamped his mouth shut. His jaw twitched.

Ignoring him, Hirdos said, "Snow, get on your hands and knees, as though we're about to mate." He gave her an intimate smile. Lowering his voice, he added, "I want to hear you cry out with pleasure."

She did as he requested. Her heavy breasts tingled, hanging free. Her pussy throbbed, aching to be filled.

Hirdos' palms molded onto her buttocks, caressing and parting them. A moan broke from her throat.

She glanced at Ryus, lying on his side a few feet away. His eyes shut as though he were in pain. His fists clenched. His cock, swollen and dark, strained against the cord.

He opened his eyes. He wasn't looking at her face but at what Hirdos was doing behind her. His chest rose and fell rapidly.

Hirdos' fingers spread her wide. Then his wet tongue swirled along her labia. She cried out, mindlessly trying to open her legs farther.

"Do it again!" she pleaded. Yes, this was what she wanted, what she ached for—a tongue pleasuring her, thrusting into her channel like a thick cock. She rocked back against him, begging wordlessly for more.

Her wild cries of delight were embarrassing but she couldn't stop herself as she rose to new heights of sensual pleasure. She gasped, pushing frantically against his tongue.

His fingers went to her labia, tracing them gently, while his tongue moved to her anus, swirling around and around, delighting nerves she'd never realized she had. His curled tongue pushed inside her puckered hole, too wet and soft to hurt. She felt as though she was rushing toward a climax, her nerves on fire.

Then his thumb fondled her swollen clit.

The sensations peaked and she exploded, her channel pulsing hard. She sobbed, her anus pulsing, her clit throbbing.

Lost in a fog of pleasure, she was barely able to stretch out onto her back. She gasped for breath, still feeling the tremors radiating through her pussy. Lying beside her, Hirdos licked her neck.

"Enough," Ryus growled.

Raising his head, Hirdos glared at him. Fearing a fight would break out, she gave Hirdos' cheek a quick caress. "Thank you," she murmured. "I've never been given such pleasure by any Earth man."

His angry look easing, he caught her hand and licked the palm. Moving away from her, he made an ironic gesture toward Ryus. *Go ahead – your turn.*

Snow relished their jealousy, their competitiveness. On Earth, she'd admired handsome, muscular men. But she'd never been desired by them. On this ship, two of the top males were ready to fight for the privilege of becoming her husband.

Ryus eased down beside her, taking her in his arms. She sighed happily, breathing in his minty scent. Being held by him was like coming home.

"Ready for more pleasure?" he asked.

Surprisingly, she was. Her pussy clenched at the rumble of his voice. The pleasure Hirdos had given her, exquisite though it had been, had left her only briefly satisfied. She wanted more.

"Touch me," she pleaded, aware of his hard cock pressing against her stomach. She ached to have him thrusting inside her pussy.

But he had to give her pleasure without mating. Well, she was ready for that.

He whispered, "Open your legs." When she moved her thighs apart, he began stroking her, the tips of his fingers playing lightly across her labia. She arched up against him, demanding a firmer touch.

He lowered his head, taking her earlobe in his teeth, nibbling it. She stretched her neck, sighing with ecstasy. His tongue teased her ear, swirling over the whorl, stroking the lobe. Meanwhile his hand touched her pussy gently, a caress that made her arch up under his fingers.

"Ryus—Ryus—" She wanted to beg but words had left her.

"Hush, Snow." He pressed the heel of his hand against her mound. Delight darted through her. Yes, the firmer touch was wonderful.

He spoke into her ear. "Want to give you more pleasure than you've ever had before."

Yes, yes, yes.

Burying his face in her neck, he bit her shoulder. Her blood leapt in response.

He stroked her labia again. She shuddered with lust, feeling his touch from her pussy all the way down to her toes. "More," she begged. If she couldn't have his cock right now, she wanted his fingers.

Taking her right nipple in his mouth, he sucked hard. At the same moment, he thrust two fingers into her hot, needy channel.

Nothing had ever felt so good.

He moved out and thrust again. She hadn't known pleasure could double in seconds.

She screamed as a powerful climax hit with the force of a lightning bolt. He thrust again and again. She thrashed her hips in rhythm with his movement. The waves of rolling ecstasy seemed to last forever. Tears welled in her eyes and spilled down her cheeks.

She went limp. She wanted to throw her arms around his neck and tell him how much she loved him. Drowsy with pleasure, she was too drained to speak.

Ryus kissed her lips, murmuring her name.

Her lids fluttered open. She gazed into his eyes. The glints of gold made her think of the sun. The glow of his eyes would surely warm her throughout her life.

"Snow, it's time to make your choice," Hirdos said.

She blinked. She'd forgotten he was there.

Releasing her, Ryus leapt to his feet, then offered his hand. She rose, facing the two gorgeous males who had just given her supremely powerful orgasms.

"Snow," Hirdos said, "if you choose me, I'll make you happy. You'll be a Council member's wife, the highest position a female can attain. My wealth will buy you all the jewelry and clothing that females delight in." He touched her face. "And now you know that I can give you pleasure as well."

"Thank you, Hirdos," she said politely. "Your offer is tempting." She turned to Ryus.

Planting his feet, he raised her chin and looked into her eyes. "Little one, I promise you this. If our mating is unsuccessful, I'll give you more time."

"You can't! The Council said—"

"If you're exiled, I'll stay with you on Jahariz."

Snow gasped, not sure she'd heard correctly. He'd give up the great venture? Go to the planet he'd described as a dismal swamp, for *her* sake?

Judging from Hirdos' poleaxed expression, Ryus had shocked him too.

Her eyes filled with tears. "Do you…can you really mean it?"

His hand flew to his right shoulder.

Gulping, she turned a questioning glance to Hirdos.

Pain filled his eyes. "I can't offer the same. As a Council member, my duty is to *Ecstasy of Generations*."

At least he'd given her a graceful way to make her choice more palatable for him. Not that there'd ever been any question in her mind.

"Hirdos?" Her throat clogged at his disappointed expression. He'd already guessed that he'd lost. "I'm sorry. Ryus is my choice."

She looked away from him. Ryus met her gaze. His eyes blazed with the light of an exploding sun.

Hirdos squared his shoulders. Gracious in defeat, he said, "I wish you both the blessings of the Great Fur-Mother." With a sad smile, he added, "And now I had better go find a Bride." Quickly he turned away, then broke into a fast lope.

"Good running," Ryus called after him. Putting his hands on Snow's shoulders, he smiled. "Now, my beautiful Snow — shall we mate?"

Goldus' words flitted through her mind. *Don't make it too easy for them, Brides!*

Grinning, she said, "If you can catch me!" She leapt away and ran, as fast as an Earthian vixen with a hunting pack after her.

Glancing behind, she saw that it took him a moment to start after her. Perhaps he hadn't believed she would flee. She lengthened her strides. She'd never been able to run so fast on Earth, not even at her peak physical strength in her early twenties.

In a few moments she heard Ryus pounding after her. Fast though she was now, she was no match for his long legs and superior strength. Catching her around the waist, he rolled to the ground, holding her on top of him.

She tried to pull away, laughing with sheer excitement. Turning, he pinned her facedown, his muscular thighs holding her while he untied the cord that held his cock. She struggled halfheartedly, knowing that was her duty as a female during the Spring Running. But what she really wanted was to mate as soon as possible.

"Love you, Snow," he said.

She stilled abruptly. He'd ever said those words before.

"Tell me you love me," he demanded. He moved off her. She raised her hips in the mating position. A moment later, she felt his hot length pressing against her entrance.

"I'll tell you after we've mated," she said. Why did she want to tease him? Perhaps because he was being foolish. Didn't he know how much she loved him? Hadn't she chosen him over a Council member?

"Tell me. Tell me *now*." He thrust inside her, the hard plunge of his cock leaving her breathless. Pleasure overtook her immediately. A climax rippled through her. She couldn't speak, could only moan with utter satisfaction.

"Love you, Snow. Love you." His thrusts quickened. "My beautiful one. Tell me. Say you love me." His voice sounded desperate.

His minty scent intensified. His ragged breathing filled her ears. The pleasure he'd given her earlier was a flickering candle compared to the raging fire of this mating.

Her pussy gushed around his driving rod. A second climax built on the heels of the first. As it reached a crescendo, she cried out, "Ryus, I love you!" Her inner muscles squeezed his powerful cock.

Ryus gripped her hips. Her sweet vagina clung around his penis as though molded to fit him.

Then the pressure suddenly increased. The tight grip of her inner muscles fueled his climax. His seed, dammed for so long, shot forth. He roared with astounded delight.

He was caught in a storm of lust, barely aware of Snow pushing back against him, ensnared in her own joy. His head whirled. How could pleasure last this long? He never wanted to stop thrusting into her.

He spurted into her again and again. Mindless with ecstasy, out of control, he rocked into her. He groaned with each long thrust.

Her vagina responded, squeezing and milking him. He reached around, rubbing his thumb against her swollen clitoris. She screamed and he felt another orgasm ripple through her.

At last his climax ebbed. Exhausted he rolled onto his side, bringing Snow down with him, still joined.

When he recovered he would mate with her again. Enticing positions flickered through his mind. He could hardly wait to take her. His penis stirred at the thought of possessing her, proving once more that she belonged to him.

He licked the back of her neck. She shivered in response.

"We mated!" Her voice rang out exultantly. "Now I don't have to be exiled!"

He tightened his grip. "My own little one," he whispered.

His left hand was on her waist. Her hand stole under his, nestling there—just as this lovely, courageous Earth woman would nestle in his heart forever.

With the last of his strength, he breathed into her ear, "I love you...my beautiful, beautiful wife."

Also by Solange Ayre

eBooks:

Bride's Holiday Gift
Ellora's Cavemen: Flavors of Ecstasy I (*anthology*)
Ellora's Cavemen: Jewels of the Nile III (*anthology*)
Emerald Eyes
Wizard's Woman

Print Books:

Ellora's Cavemen: Flavors of Ecstasy I (*anthology*)
Ellora's Cavemen: Jewels of the Nile III (*anthology*)
Erotic Emerald (*anthology*)
Tempting Treats (*anthology*)

About the Author

༙

Solange Ayre, galaxy-hopping investigative journalist, also serves as a policy advisor to the United Conglomeration of Planetary Jurisdictions. She makes her home on Ayriana, her private island-republic in the West Caribbean region of Earth.

After a whirlwind childhood living in the capitals of Europe, Solange married St. Georges Ayre, one of the wealthiest men in the world. The crystal palace he bought her on Ayriana is the primary tourist attraction in the area--at least, for those who can find it. St. George's mysterious assassination is still mourned by his grieving widow.

Directly descended from King Louis XVI and Marie Antoinette, Solange graciously supports the democratic government of France and relinquishes her claim to the throne. Under no circumstances will she answer to the title "Your Highness."

In her spare time, Solange enjoys breeding and showing her prize-winning miniature dragons as well as researching and writing erotic romance.

Solange welcomes comments from readers. You can find her website and email address on her author bio page at www.ellorascave.com.

Tell Us What You Think

We appreciate hearing reader opinions about our books. You can email us at Comments@EllorasCave.com.

Why an electronic book?

We live in the Information Age—an exciting time in the history of human civilization, in which technology rules supreme and continues to progress in leaps and bounds every minute of every day. For a multitude of reasons, more and more avid literary fans are opting to purchase e-books instead of paper books. The question from those not yet initiated into the world of electronic reading is simply: *Why?*

1. ***Price.*** An electronic title at Ellora's Cave Publishing and Cerridwen Press runs anywhere from 40% to 75% less than the cover price of the exact same title in paperback format. Why? Basic mathematics and cost. It is less expensive to publish an e-book (no paper and printing, no warehousing and shipping) than it is to publish a paperback, so the savings are passed along to the consumer.

2. ***Space.*** Running out of room in your house for your books? That is one worry you will never have with electronic books. For a low one-time cost, you can purchase a handheld device specifically designed for e-reading. Many e-readers have large, convenient screens for viewing. Better yet, hundreds of titles can be stored within your new library—on a single microchip. There are a variety of e-readers from different manufacturers. You can also read e-books on your PC or laptop computer. (Please note that Ellora's Cave does not endorse any specific brands.

You can check our websites at www.ellorascave.com or www.cerridwenpress.com for information we make available to new consumers.)

3. *Mobility.* Because your new e-library consists of only a microchip within a small, easily transportable e-reader, your entire cache of books can be taken with you wherever you go.
4. *Personal Viewing Preferences.* Are the words you are currently reading too small? Too large? Too… ANNOYING? Paperback books cannot be modified according to personal preferences, but e-books can.
5. *Instant Gratification.* Is it the middle of the night and all the bookstores near you are closed? Are you tired of waiting days, sometimes weeks, for bookstores to ship the novels you bought? Ellora's Cave Publishing sells instantaneous downloads twenty-four hours a day, seven days a week, every day of the year. Our webstore is never closed. Our e-book delivery system is 100% automated, meaning your order is filled as soon as you pay for it.

Those are a few of the top reasons why electronic books are replacing paperbacks for many avid readers.

As always, Ellora's Cave and Cerridwen Press welcome your questions and comments. We invite you to email us at Comments@ellorascave.com or write to us directly at Ellora's Cave Publishing Inc., 1056 Home Avenue, Akron, OH 44310-3502.

COMING TO A BOOKSTORE NEAR YOU!

ELLORA'S CAVE

Bestselling Authors Tour

UPDATES AVAILABLE AT
WWW.ELLORASCAVE.COM

Cerridwen, the Celtic Goddess of wisdom, was the muse who brought inspiration to storytellers and those in the creative arts. Cerridwen Press encompasses the best and most innovative stories in all genres of today's fiction. Visit our site and discover the newest titles by talented authors who still get inspired - much like the ancient storytellers did, once upon a time.

Cerridwen Press
www.cerridwenpress.com

ELLORA'S CAVE
ROMANTICA PUBLISHING

Discover for yourself why readers can't get enough of the multiple award-winning publisher

Ellora's Cave.

Whether you prefer e-books or paperbacks,

be sure to visit EC on the web at
www.ellorascave.com

for an erotic reading experience that will leave you breathless.